DISNEP

MONSTERS AT WORK

Published in the United States by Random House Children's Books, a division of Penguin Random House LLC, 1745 Broadway, New York, NY, 10019, and in Canada by Penguin Random House Canada Limited, Toronto, in conjunction with Disney Enterprises, Inc. Screen Comix is a trademark of Penguin Random House LLC. Random House and the colophon are registered trademarks of Penguin Random House LLC.

rhcbooks.com

ISBN 978-0-7364-4276-3 (trade) — ISBN 978-0-7364-4277-0 (ebook)

Printed in the United States of America

10 9 8 7 6 5 4 3 2 1

Disney

MONSTERS AT WORK

Meet MIFT

Random House 🏠 New York

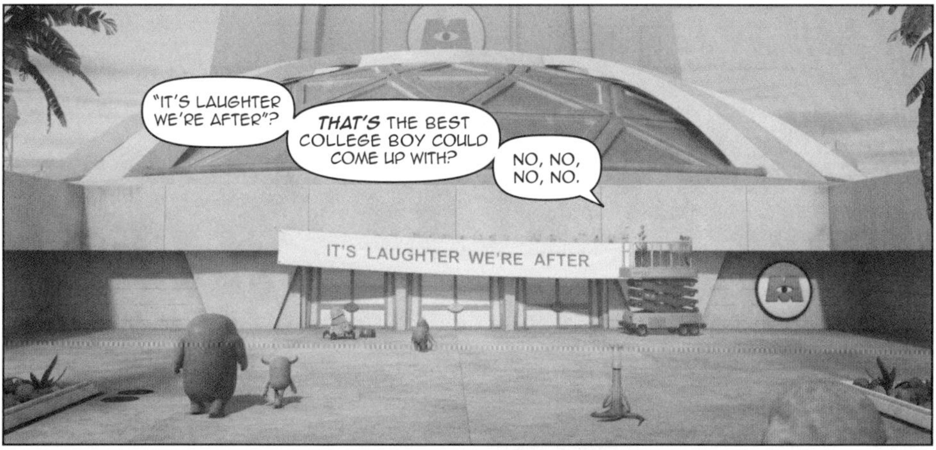
"IT'S LAUGHTER WE'RE AFTER"?
THAT'S THE BEST COLLEGE BOY COULD COME UP WITH?
NO, NO, NO, NO.
IT'S LAUGHTER WE'RE AFTER

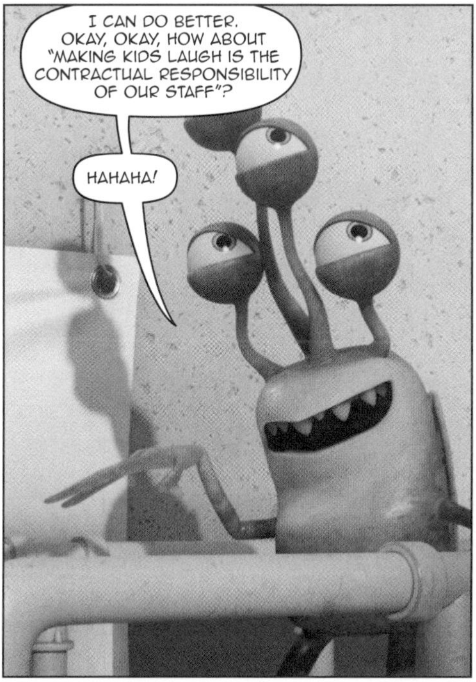
I CAN DO BETTER. OKAY, OKAY, HOW ABOUT "MAKING KIDS LAUGH IS THE CONTRACTUAL RESPONSIBILITY OF OUR STAFF"?
HAHAHA!

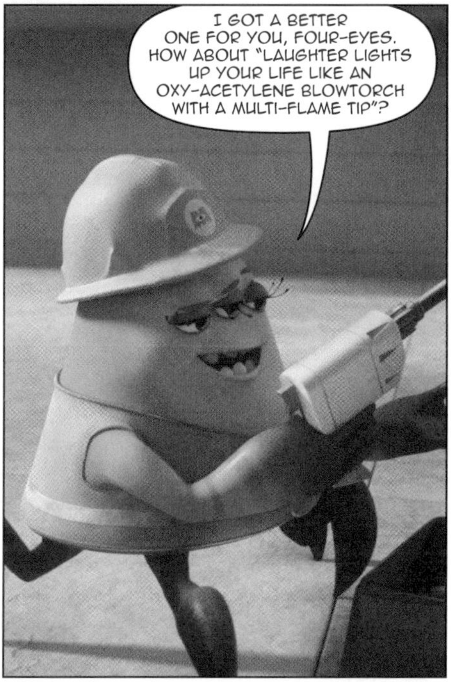
I GOT A BETTER ONE FOR YOU, FOUR-EYES. HOW ABOUT "LAUGHTER LIGHTS UP YOUR LIFE LIKE AN OXY-ACETYLENE BLOWTORCH WITH A MULTI-FLAME TIP"?

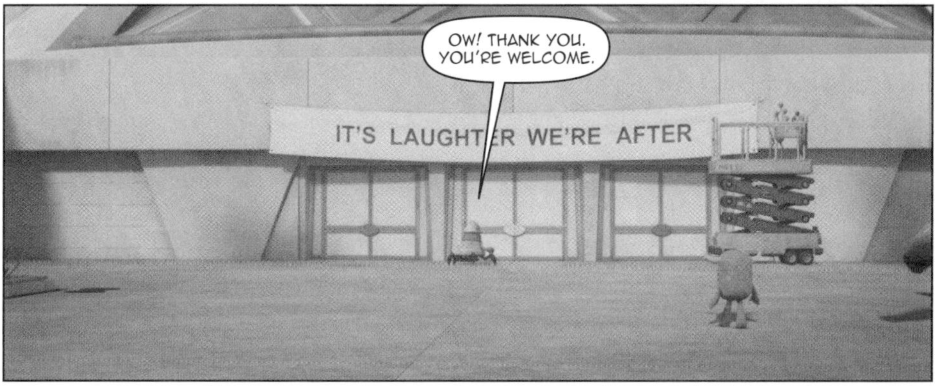
OW! THANK YOU. YOU'RE WELCOME.
IT'S LAUGHT ER WE'RE AFTER

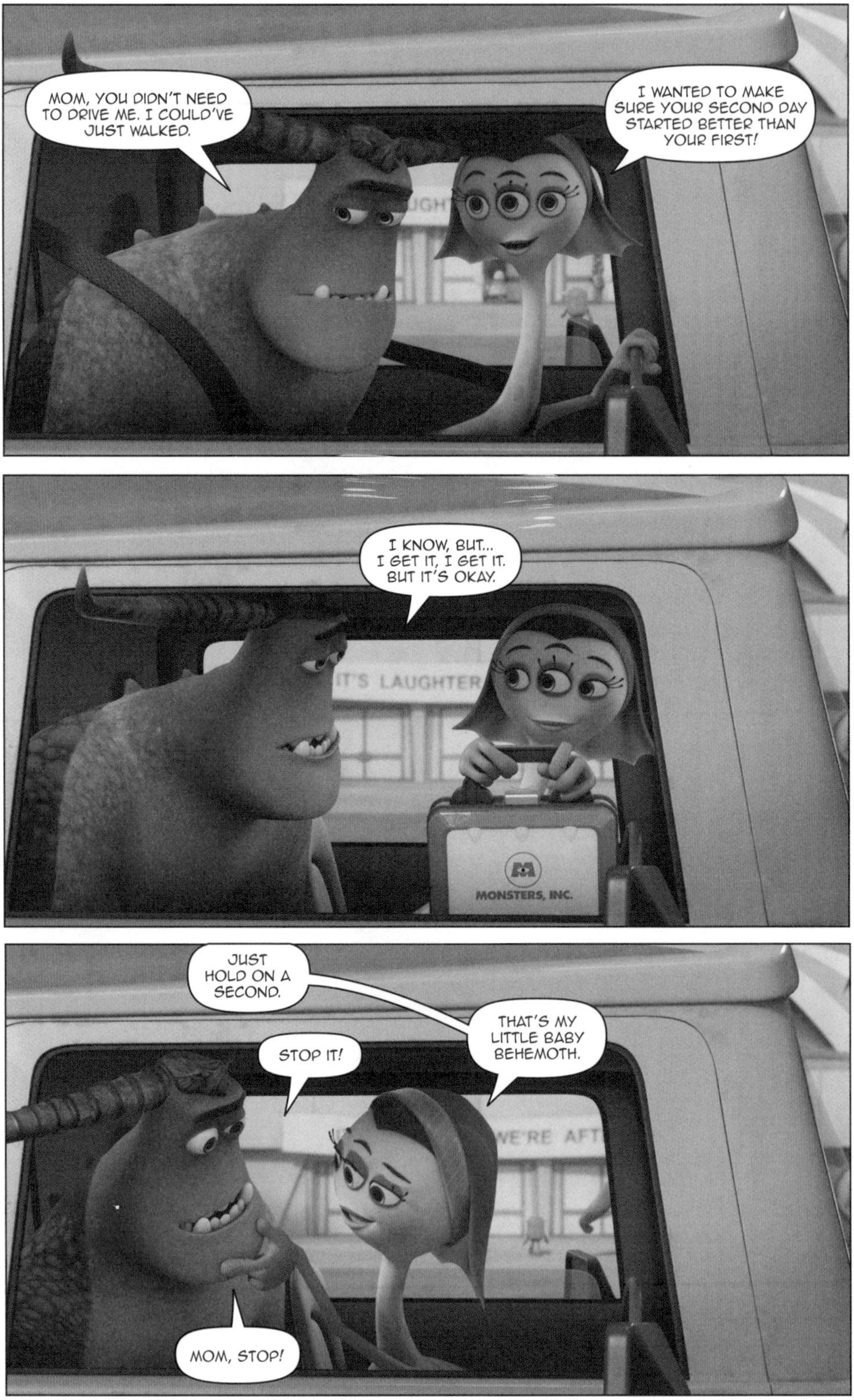
MOM, YOU DIDN'T NEED TO DRIVE ME. I COULD'VE JUST WALKED.
I WANTED TO MAKE SURE YOUR SECOND DAY STARTED BETTER THAN YOUR FIRST!
I KNOW, BUT... I GET IT, I GET IT. BUT IT'S OKAY.
MONSTERS, INC.
JUST HOLD ON A SECOND.
THAT'S MY LITTLE BABY BEHEMOTH.
STOP IT!
MOM, STOP!

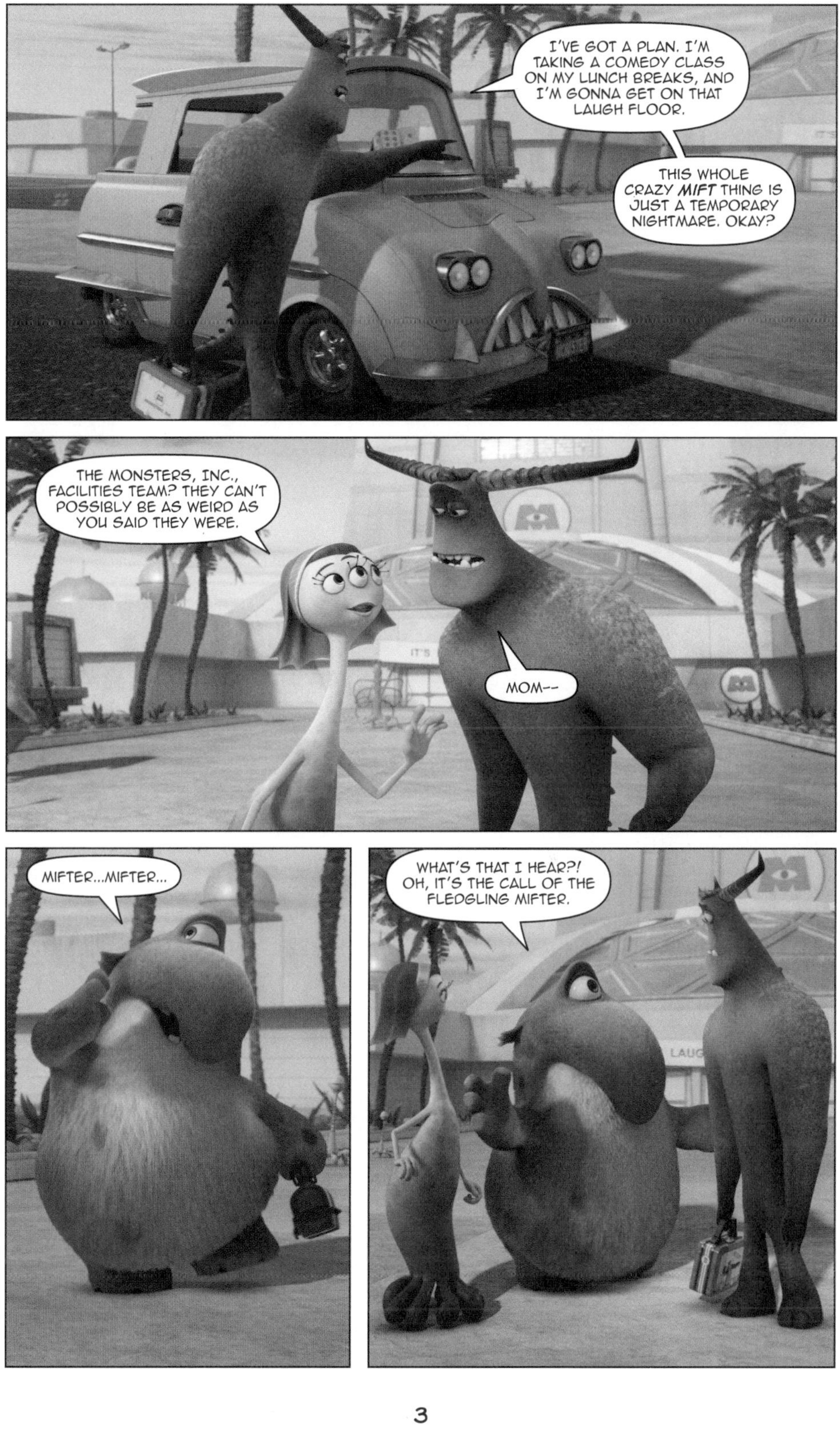
I'VE GOT A PLAN. I'M TAKING A COMEDY CLASS ON MY LUNCH BREAKS, AND I'M GONNA GET ON THAT LAUGH FLOOR.
THIS WHOLE CRAZY *MIFT* THING IS JUST A TEMPORARY NIGHTMARE. OKAY?
THE MONSTERS, INC., FACILITIES TEAM? THEY CAN'T POSSIBLY BE AS WEIRD AS YOU SAID THEY WERE.
MOM--
MIFTER...MIFTER...
WHAT'S THAT I HEAR?! OH, IT'S THE CALL OF THE FLEDGLING MIFTER.

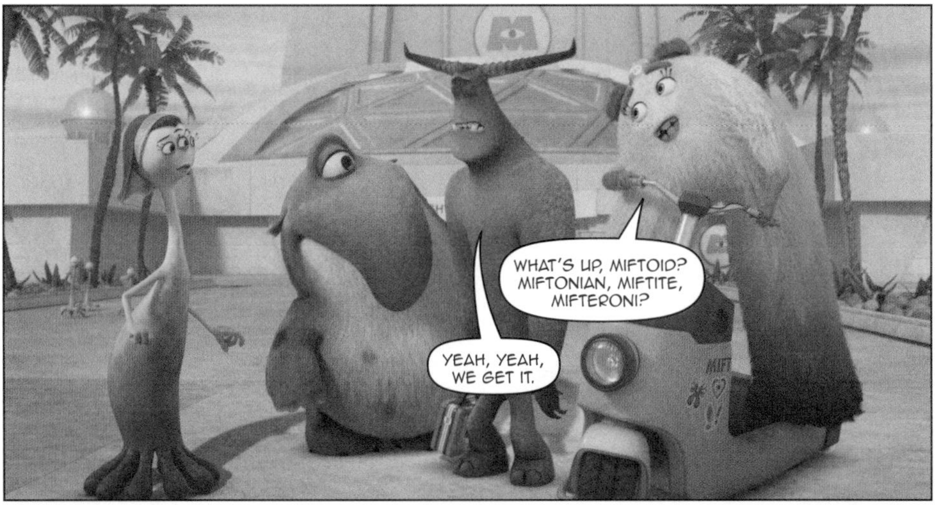
WHAT'S UP, MIFTOID? MIFTONIAN, MIFTITE, MIFTERONI?
YEAH, YEAH, WE GET IT.

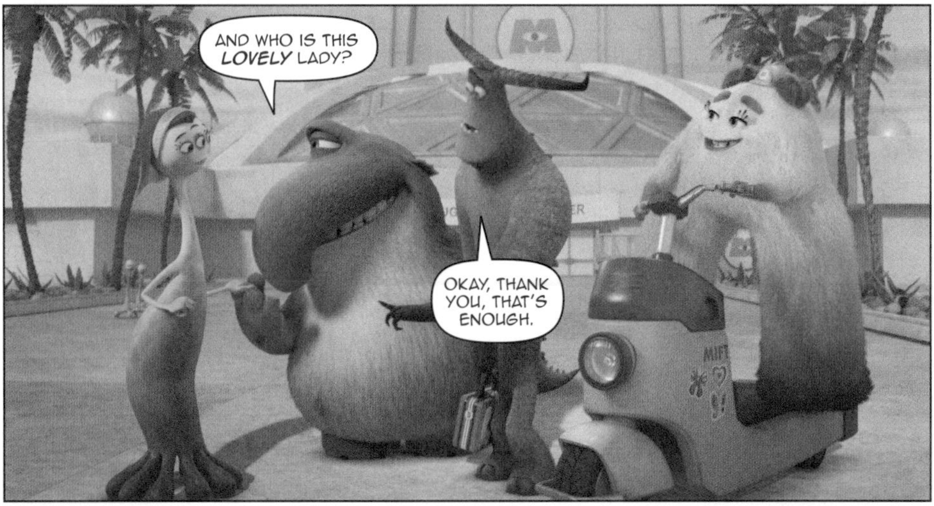
AND WHO IS THIS *LOVELY* LADY?
OKAY, THANK YOU, THAT'S ENOUGH.

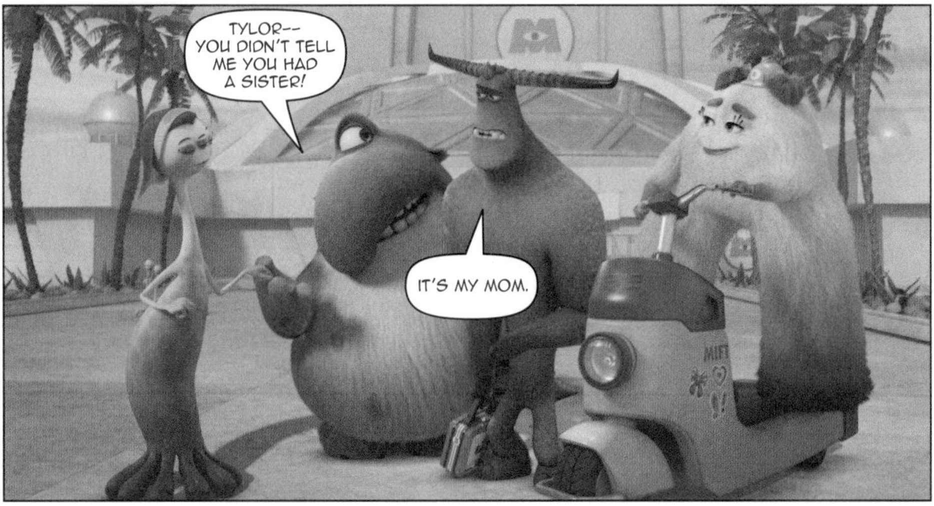
TYLOR-- YOU DIDN'T TELL ME YOU HAD A SISTER!
IT'S MY MOM.

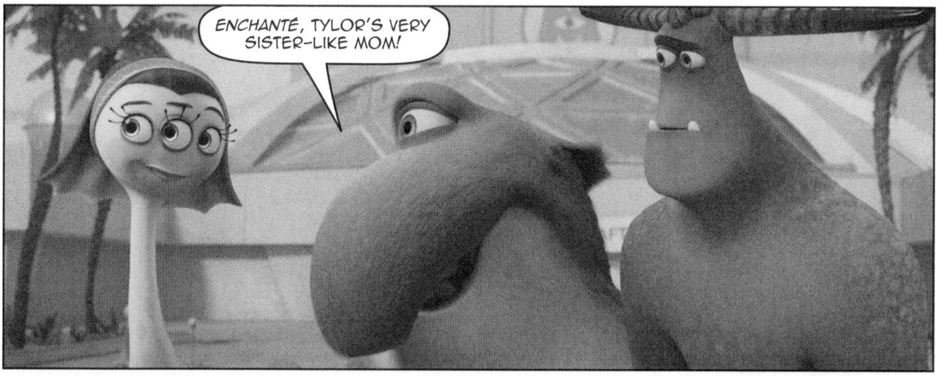
ENCHANTÉ, TYLOR'S VERY SISTER-LIKE MOM!

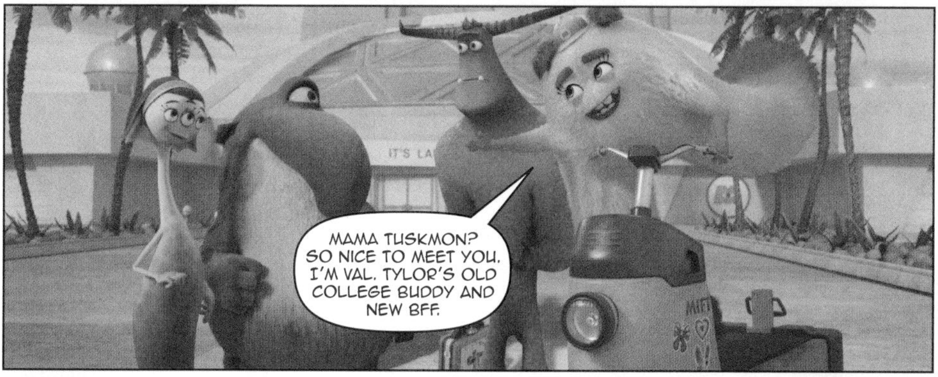
MAMA TUSKMON? SO NICE TO MEET YOU. I'M VAL. TYLOR'S OLD COLLEGE BUDDY AND NEW BFF.

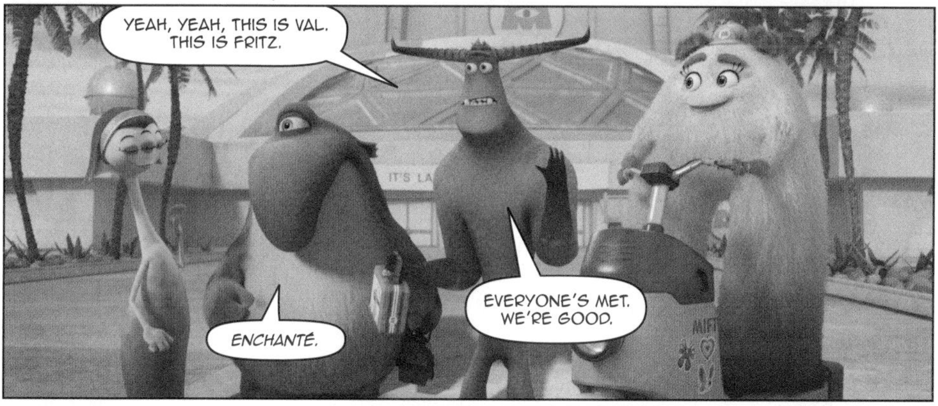
YEAH, YEAH, THIS IS VAL. THIS IS FRITZ.
ENCHANTÉ.
EVERYONE'S MET. WE'RE GOOD.

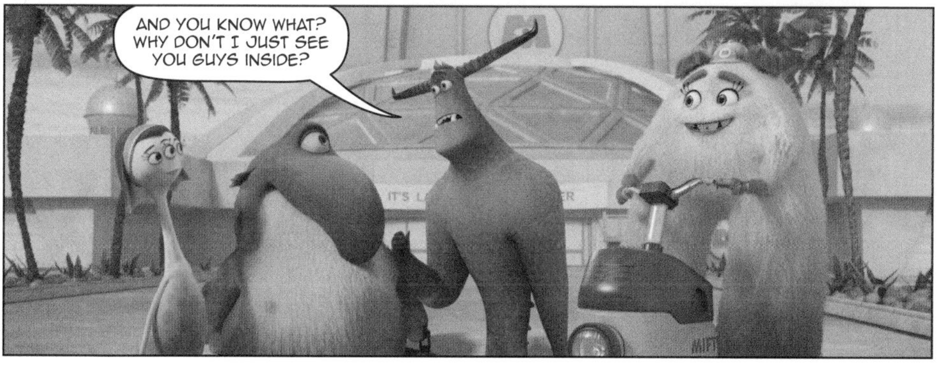
AND YOU KNOW WHAT? WHY DON'T I JUST SEE YOU GUYS INSIDE?

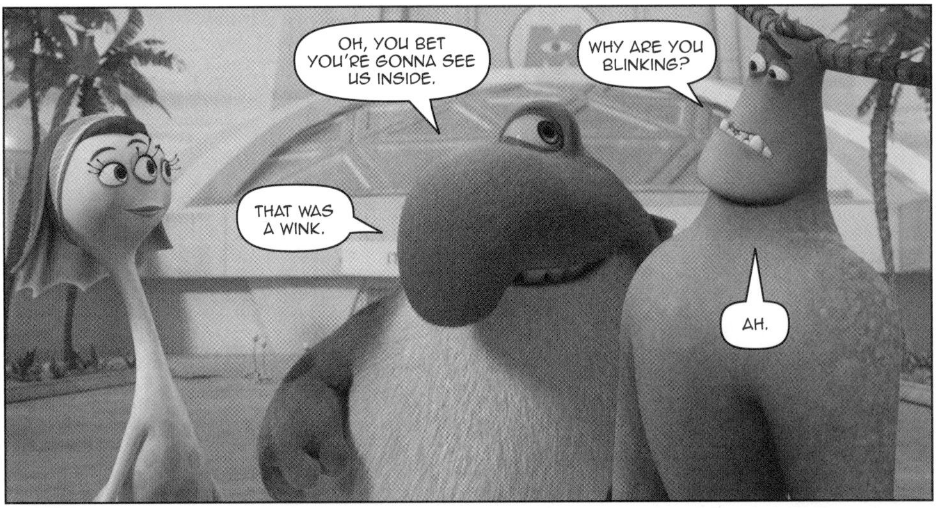
OH, YOU BET YOU'RE GONNA SEE US INSIDE.
WHY ARE YOU BLINKING?
THAT WAS A WINK.
AH.

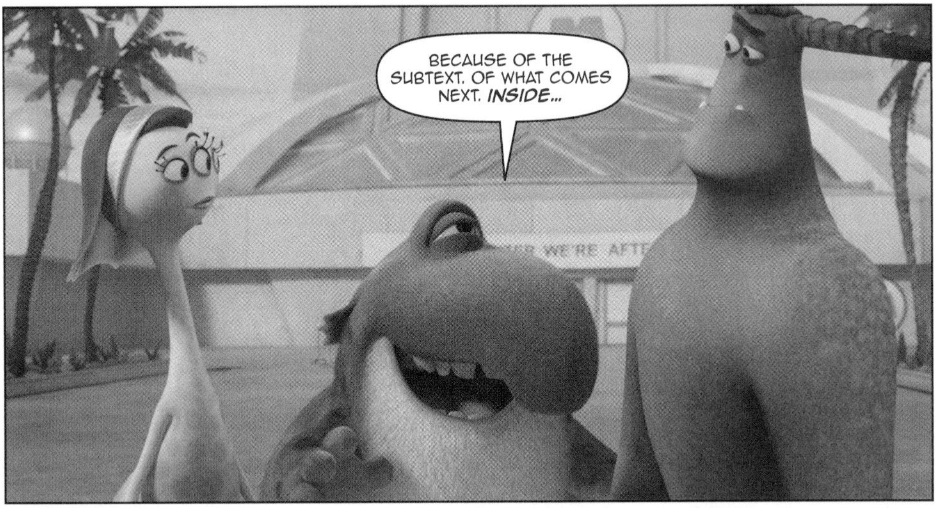
BECAUSE OF THE SUBTEXT. OF WHAT COMES NEXT. *INSIDE...*

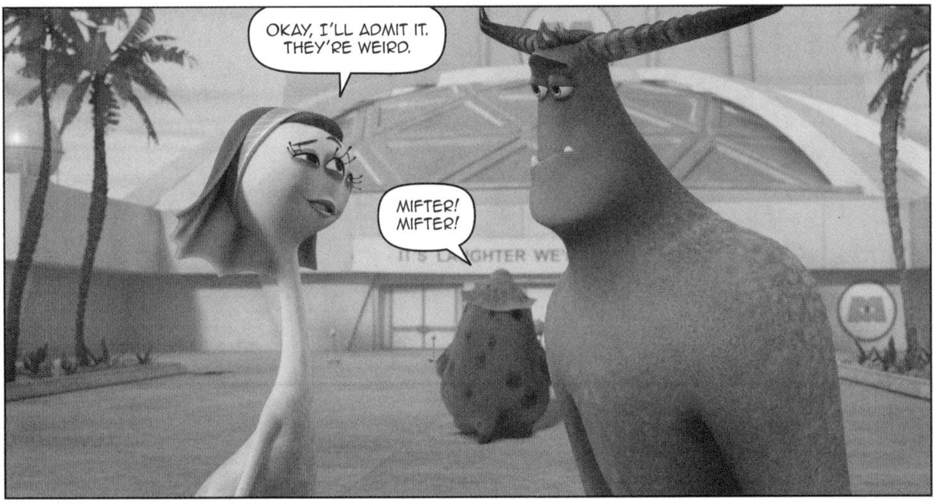
OKAY, I'LL ADMIT IT. THEY'RE WEIRD.
MIFTER! MIFTER!

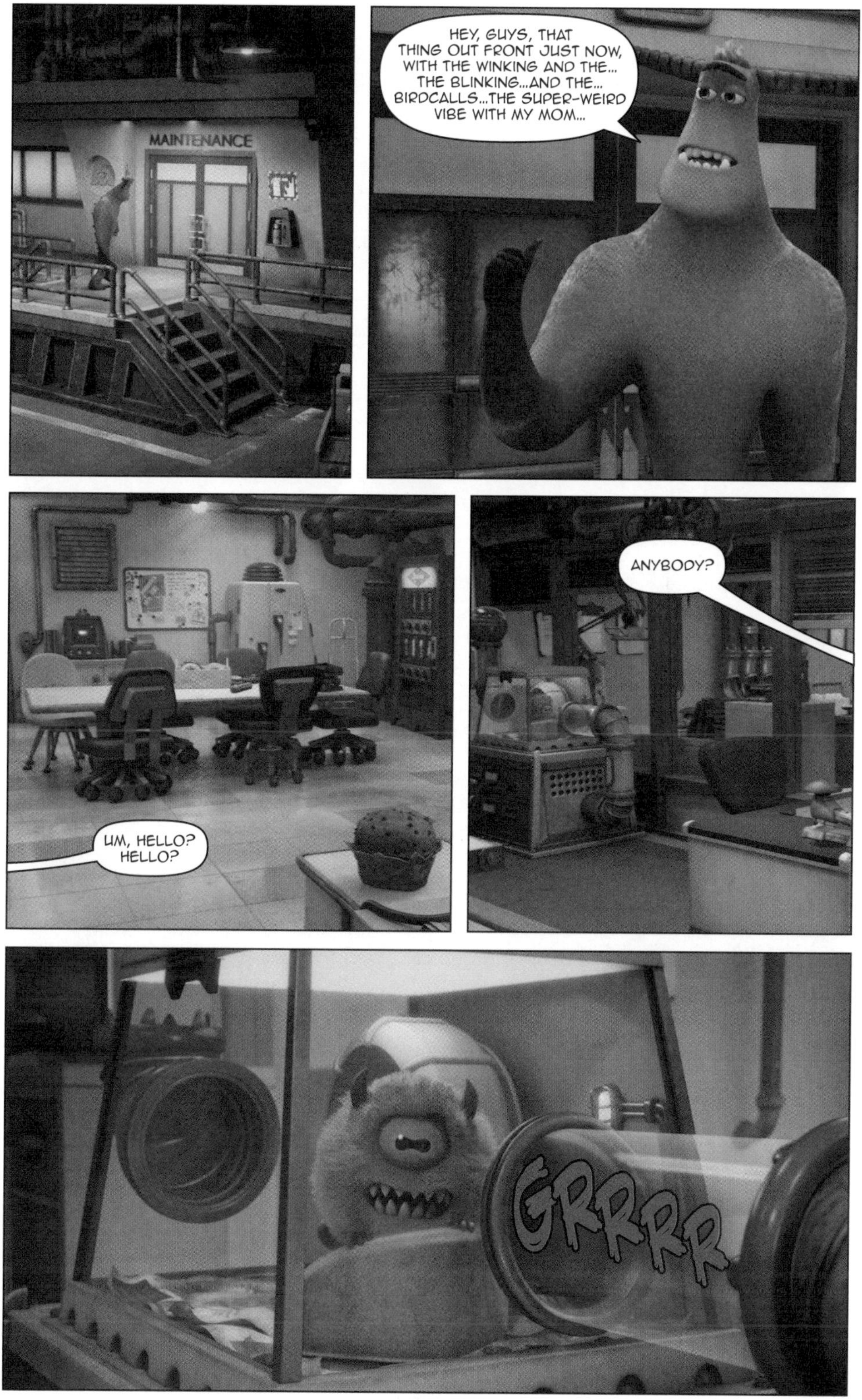
MAINTENANCE
HEY, GUYS, THAT THING OUT FRONT JUST NOW, WITH THE WINKING AND THE... THE BLINKING...AND THE... BIRDCALLS...THE SUPER-WEIRD VIBE WITH MY MOM...
UM, HELLO? HELLO?
ANYBODY?
GRRRR

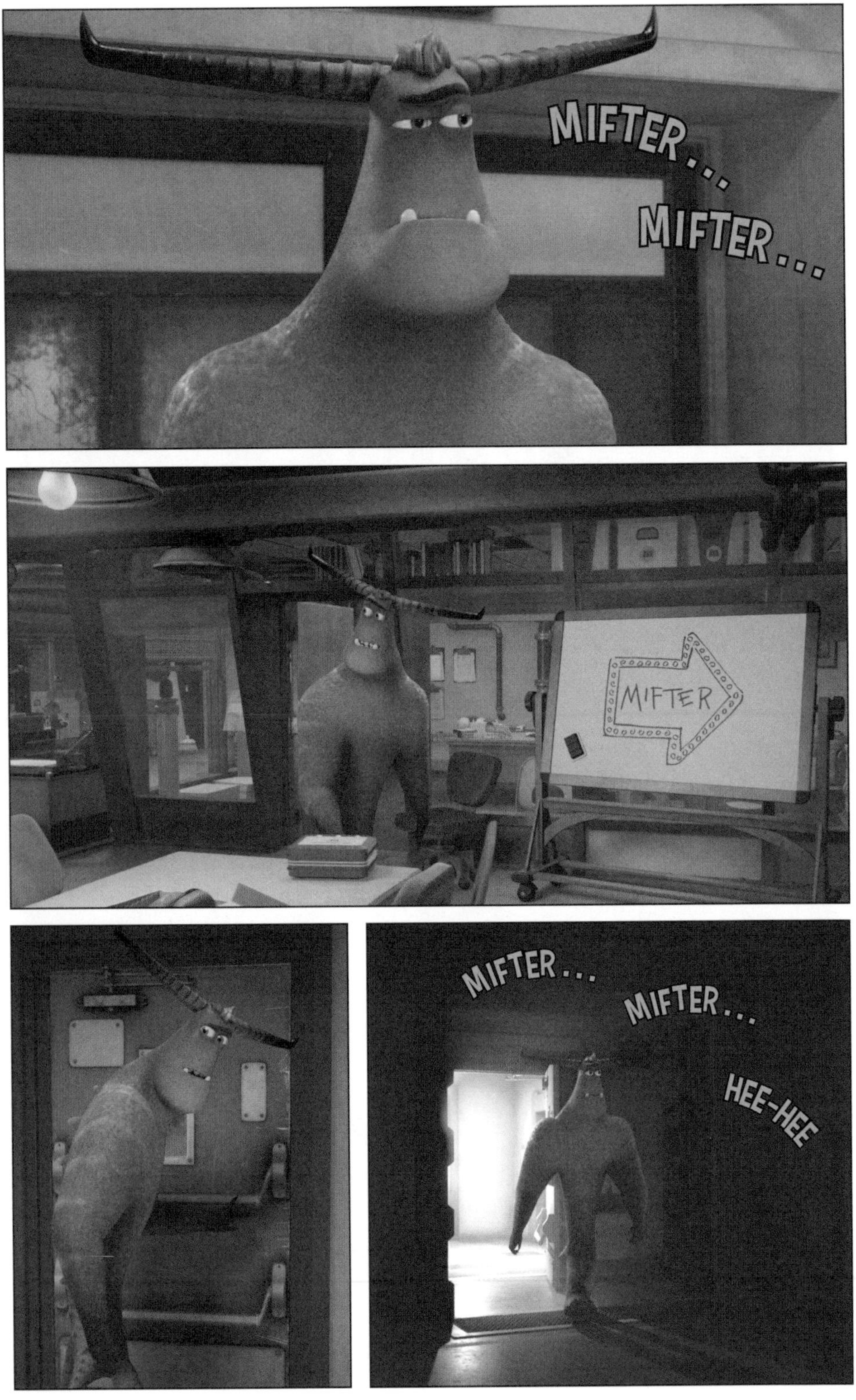
MIFTER...
MIFTER...
MIFTER
MIFTER...
MIFTER...
HEE-HEE

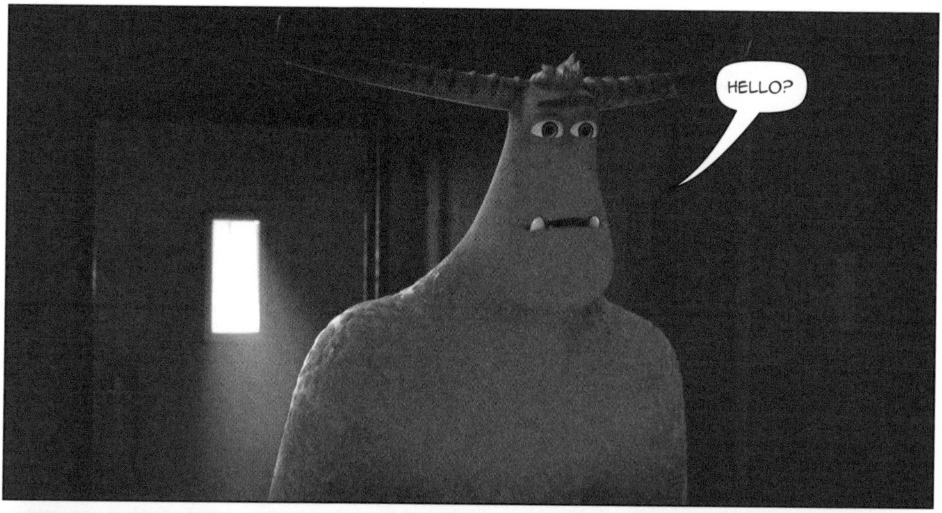
HELLO?

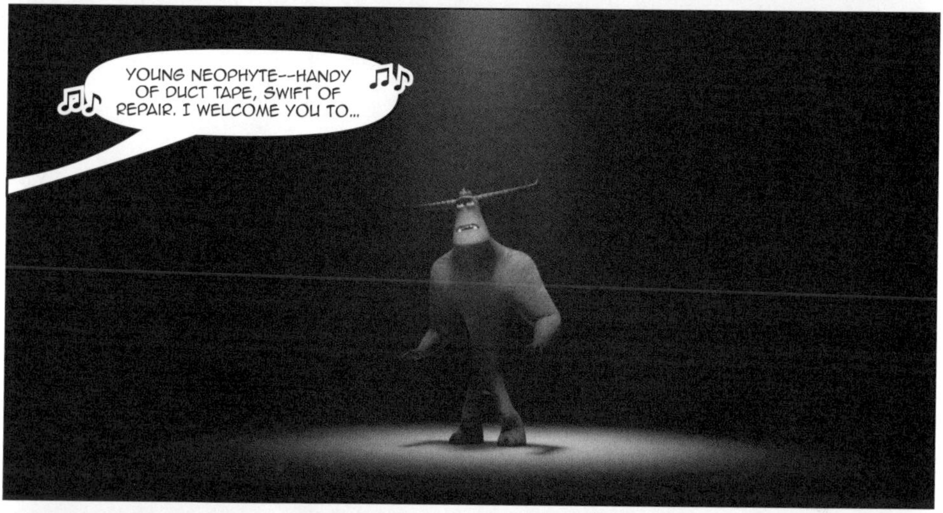
YOUNG NEOPHYTE--HANDY OF DUCT TAPE, SWIFT OF REPAIR. I WELCOME YOU TO...

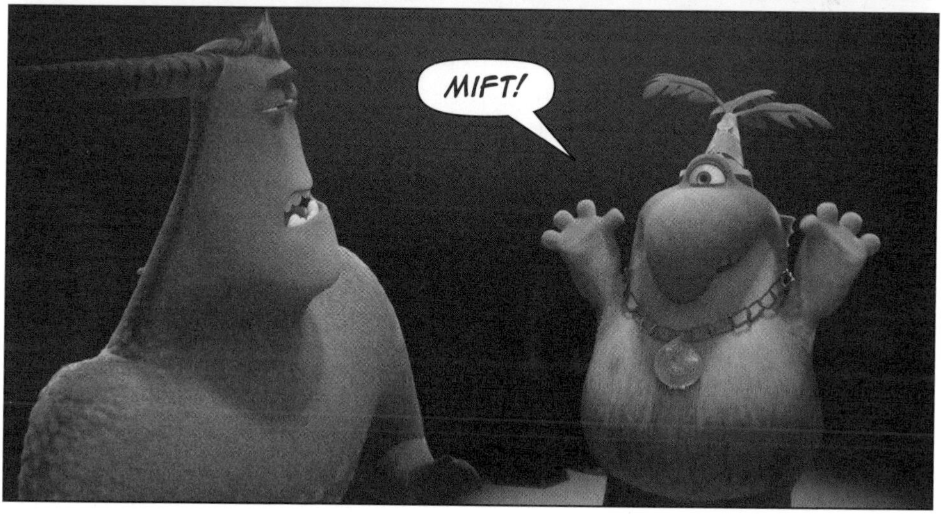
MIFT!

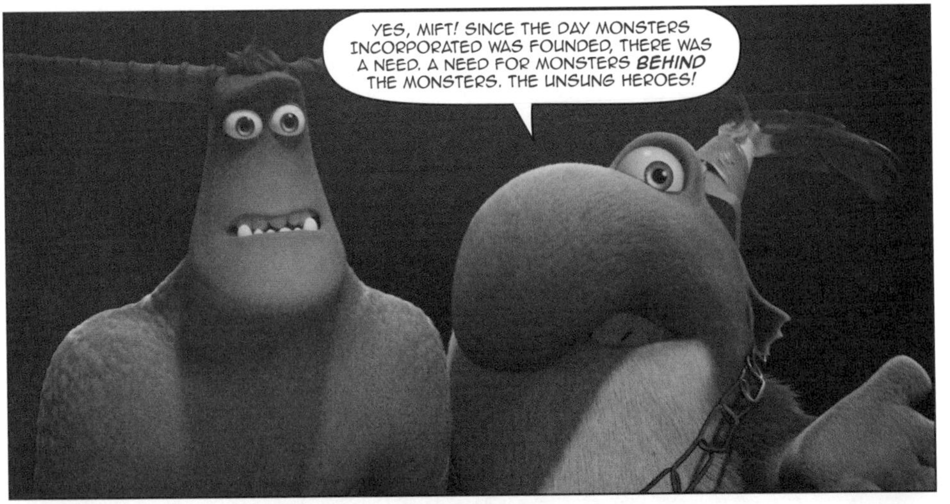
YES, MIFT! SINCE THE DAY MONSTERS INCORPORATED WAS FOUNDED, THERE WAS A NEED. A NEED FOR MONSTERS *BEHIND* THE MONSTERS. THE UNSUNG HEROES!

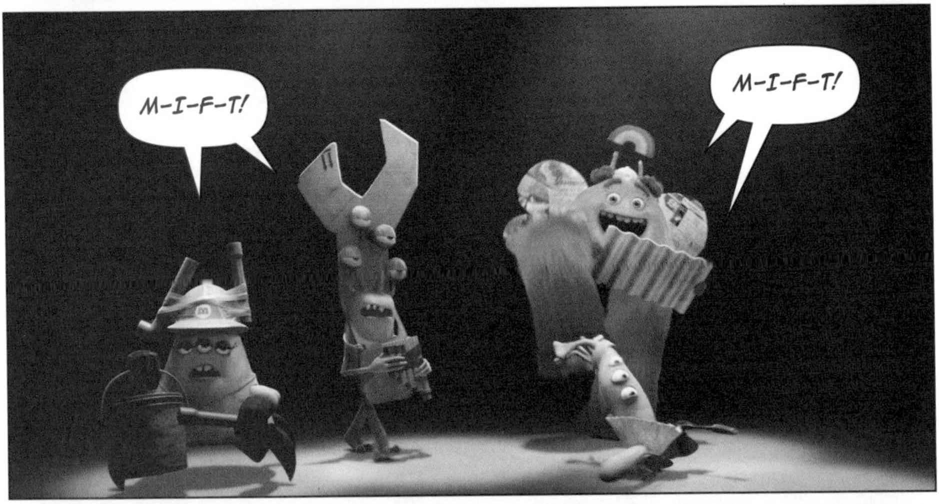
M-I-F-T!
M-I-F-T!

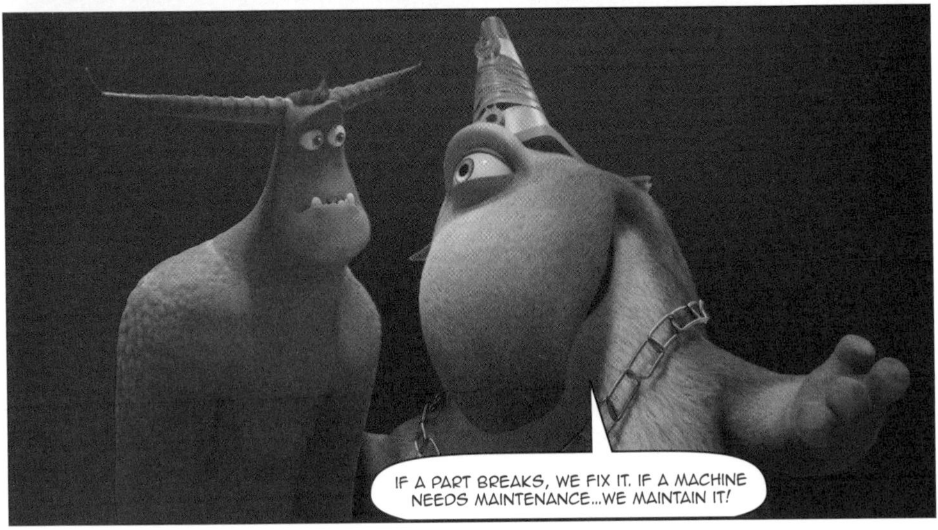
IF A PART BREAKS, WE FIX IT. IF A MACHINE NEEDS MAINTENANCE...WE MAINTAIN IT!

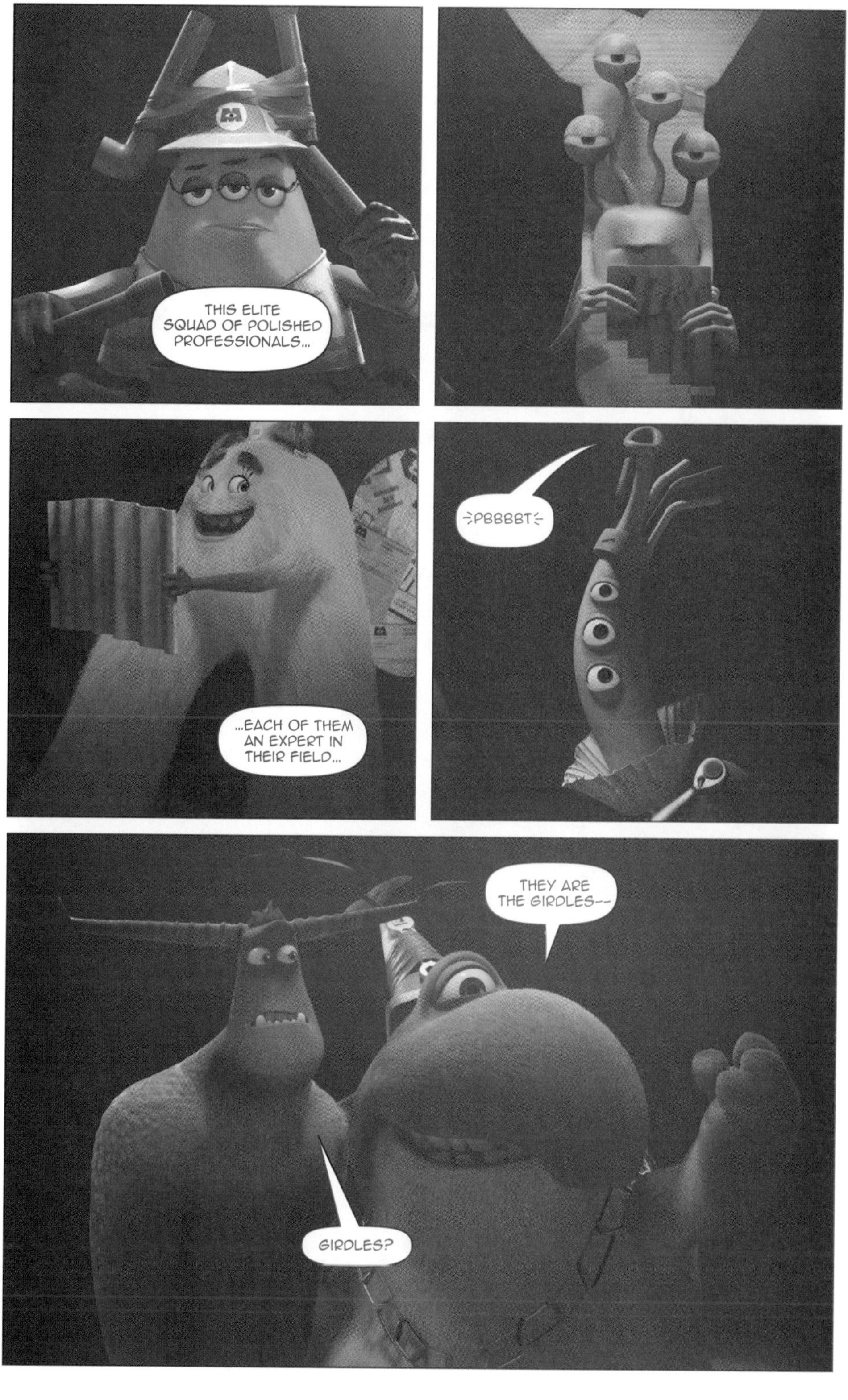
THIS ELITE SQUAD OF POLISHED PROFESSIONALS...
...EACH OF THEM AN EXPERT IN THEIR FIELD...
PBBBBT
THEY ARE THE GIRDLES--
GIRDLES?

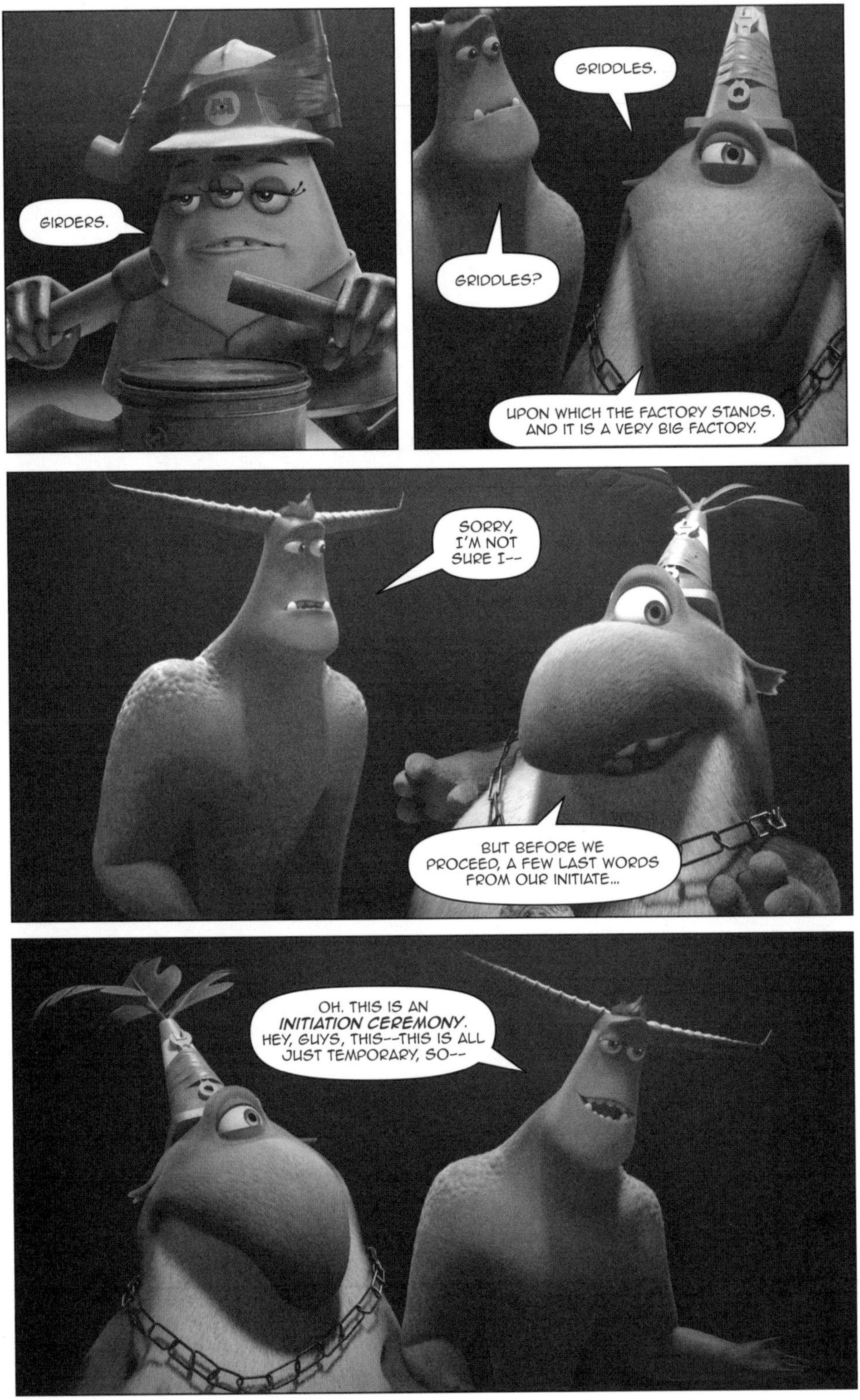
GIRDERS.
GRIDDLES.
GRIDDLES?
UPON WHICH THE FACTORY STANDS. AND IT IS A VERY BIG FACTORY.
SORRY, I'M NOT SURE I--
BUT BEFORE WE PROCEED, A FEW LAST WORDS FROM OUR INITIATE...
OH. THIS IS AN *INITIATION CEREMONY*. HEY, GUYS, THIS--THIS IS ALL JUST TEMPORARY, SO--

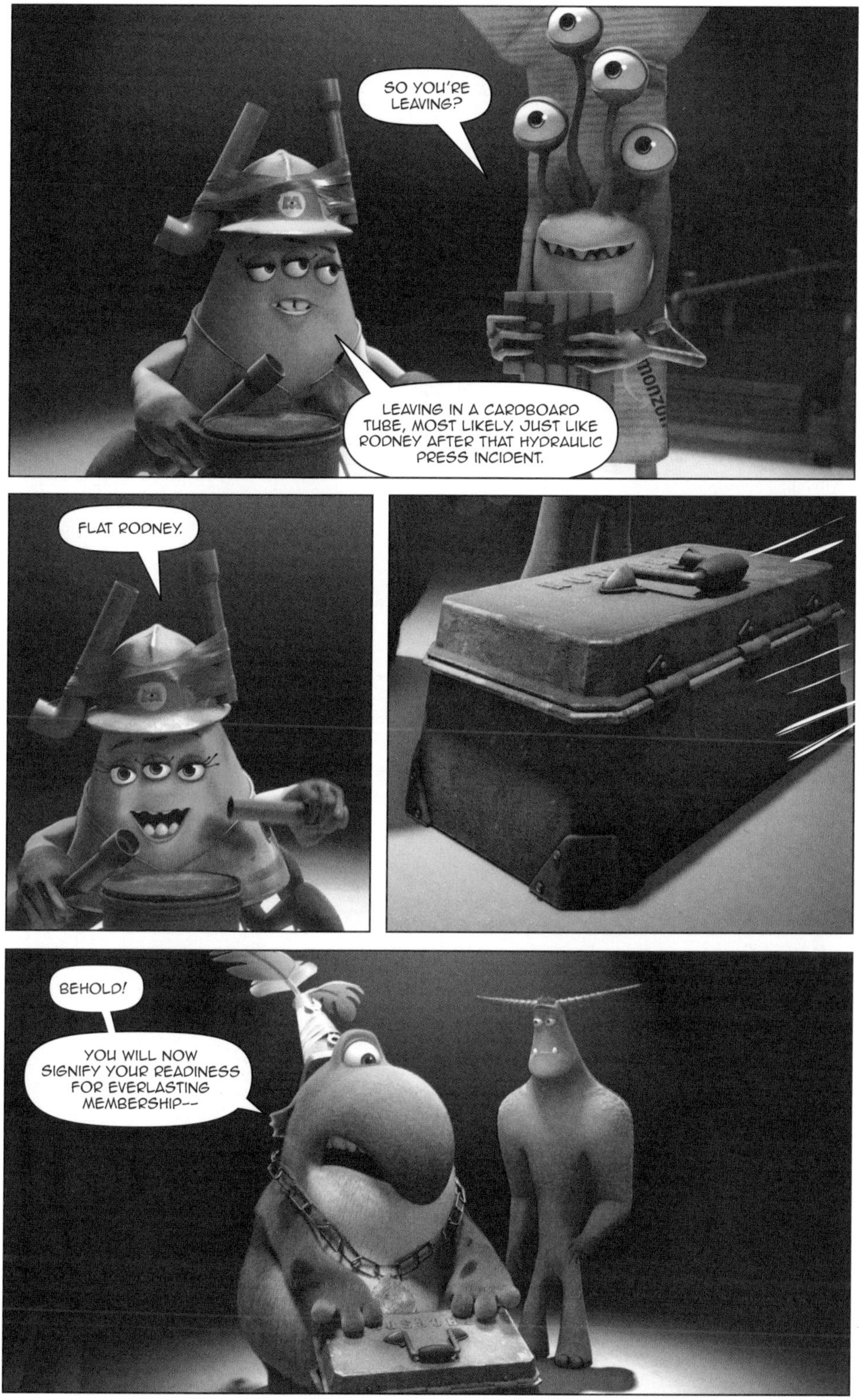
SO YOU'RE LEAVING?
LEAVING IN A CARDBOARD TUBE, MOST LIKELY. JUST LIKE RODNEY AFTER THAT HYDRAULIC PRESS INCIDENT.
FLAT RODNEY.
BEHOLD!
YOU WILL NOW SIGNIFY YOUR READINESS FOR EVERLASTING MEMBERSHIP--

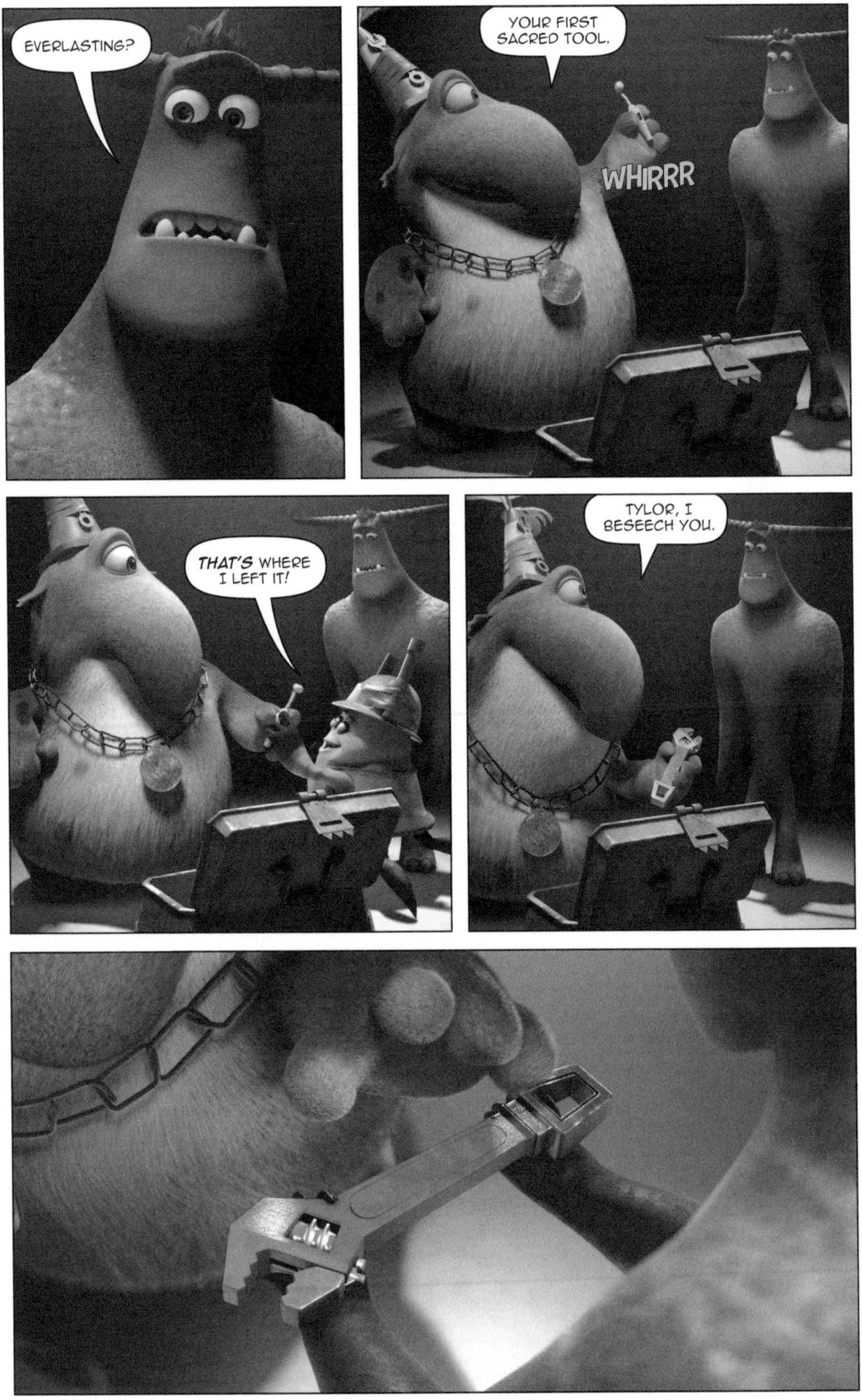
EVERLASTING?
YOUR FIRST SACRED TOOL.
WHIRRR
THAT'S WHERE I LEFT IT!
TYLOR, I BESEECH YOU.

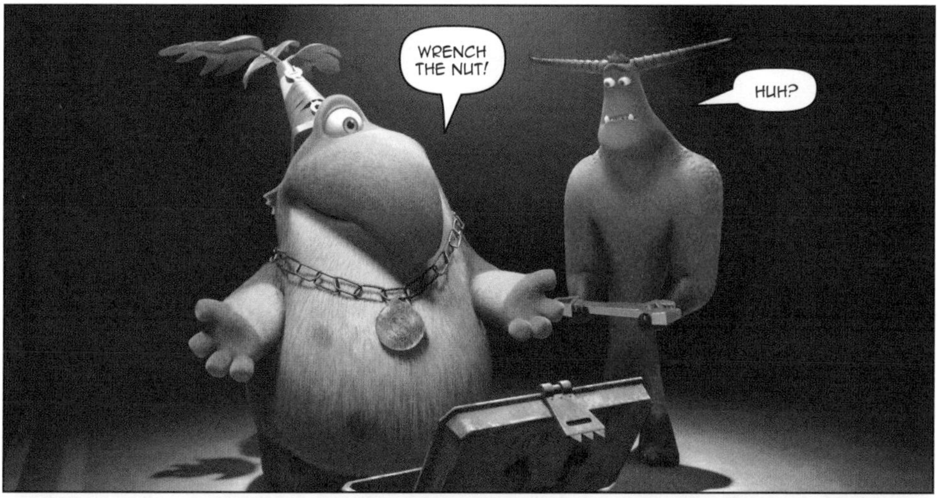
WRENCH THE NUT!
HUH?

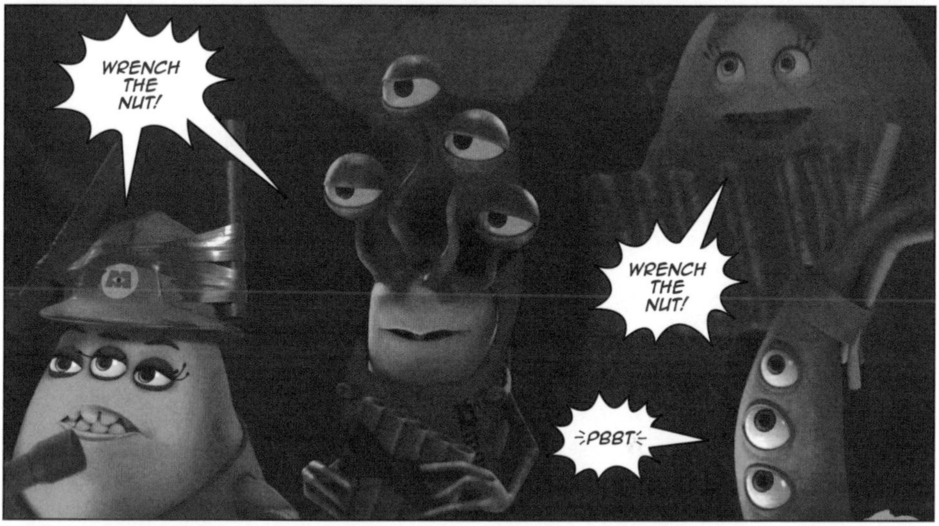
WRENCH THE NUT!
WRENCH THE NUT!
PBBT

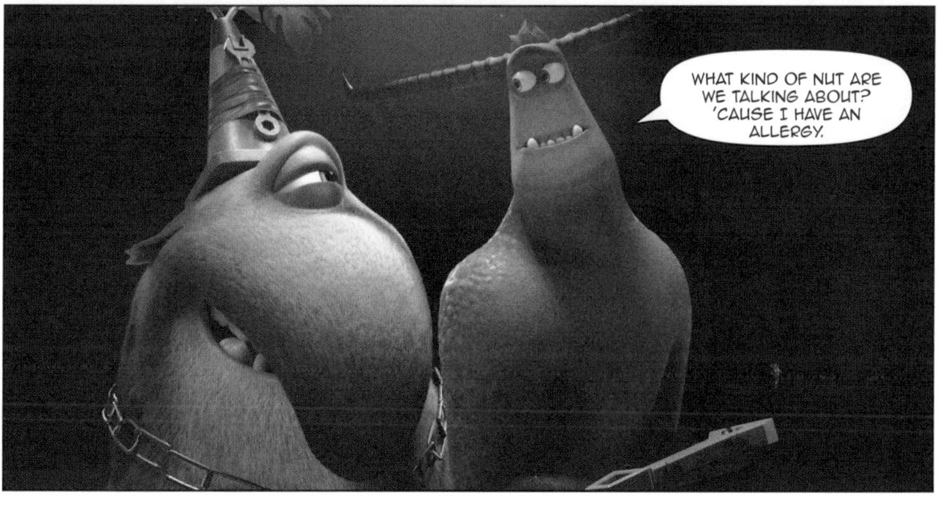
WHAT KIND OF NUT ARE WE TALKING ABOUT? 'CAUSE I HAVE AN ALLERGY.

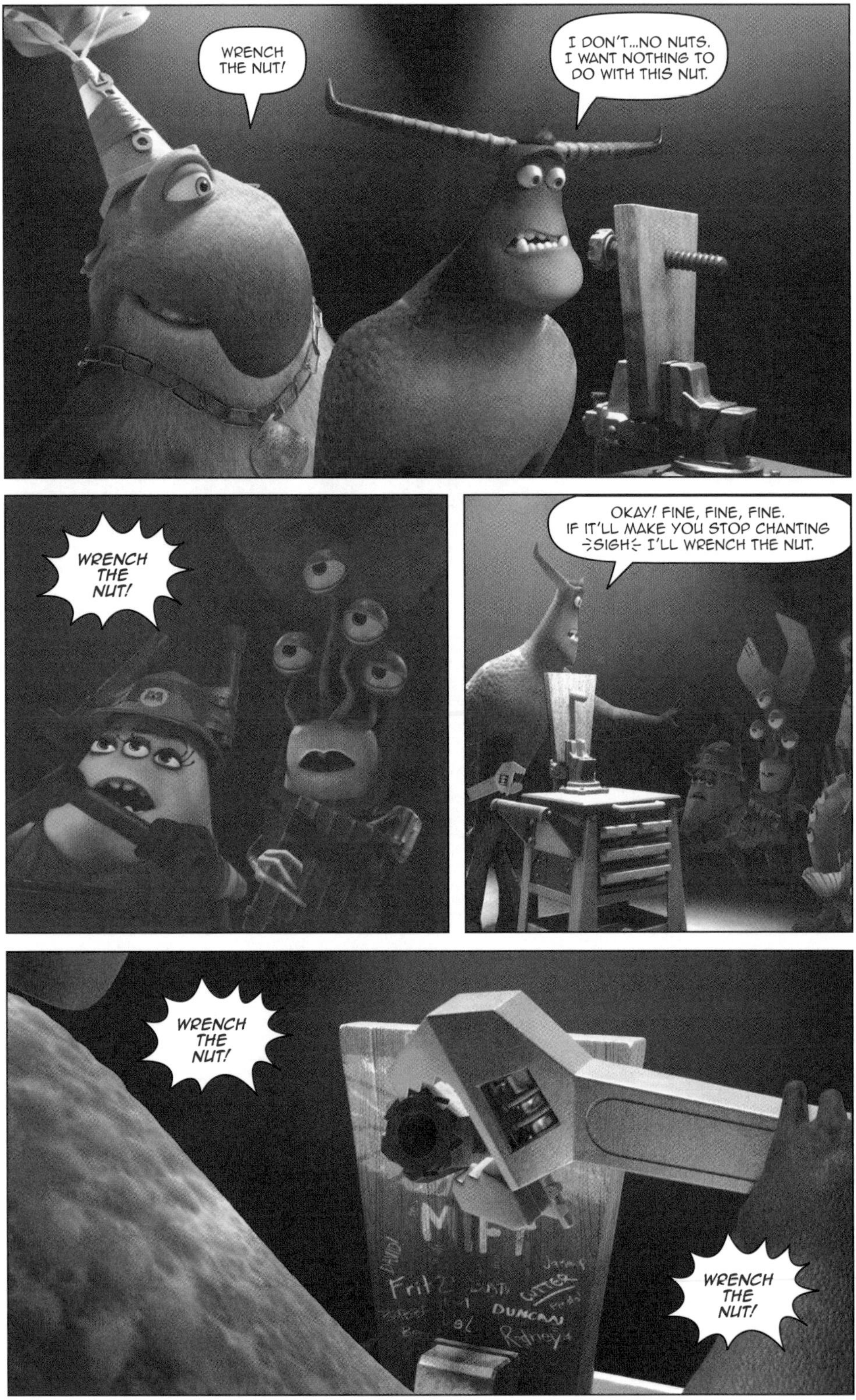

WRENCH THE NUT!
I DON'T...NO NUTS. I WANT NOTHING TO DO WITH THIS NUT.
WRENCH THE NUT!
OKAY! FINE, FINE, FINE. IF IT'LL MAKE YOU STOP CHANTING *SIGH* I'LL WRENCH THE NUT.
WRENCH THE NUT!
WRENCH THE NUT!

SQUEAK
UH-OH.

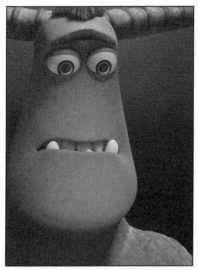

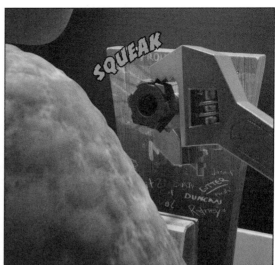

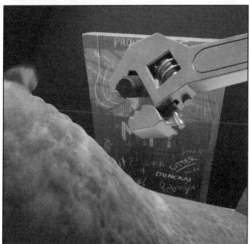

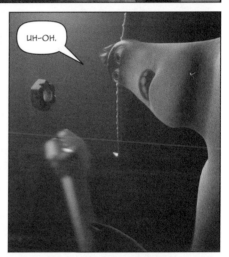

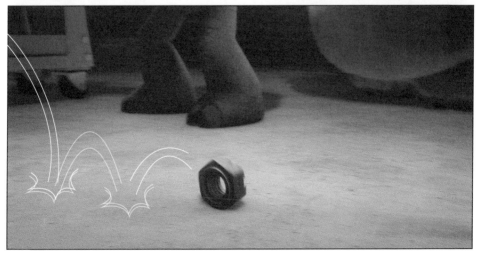

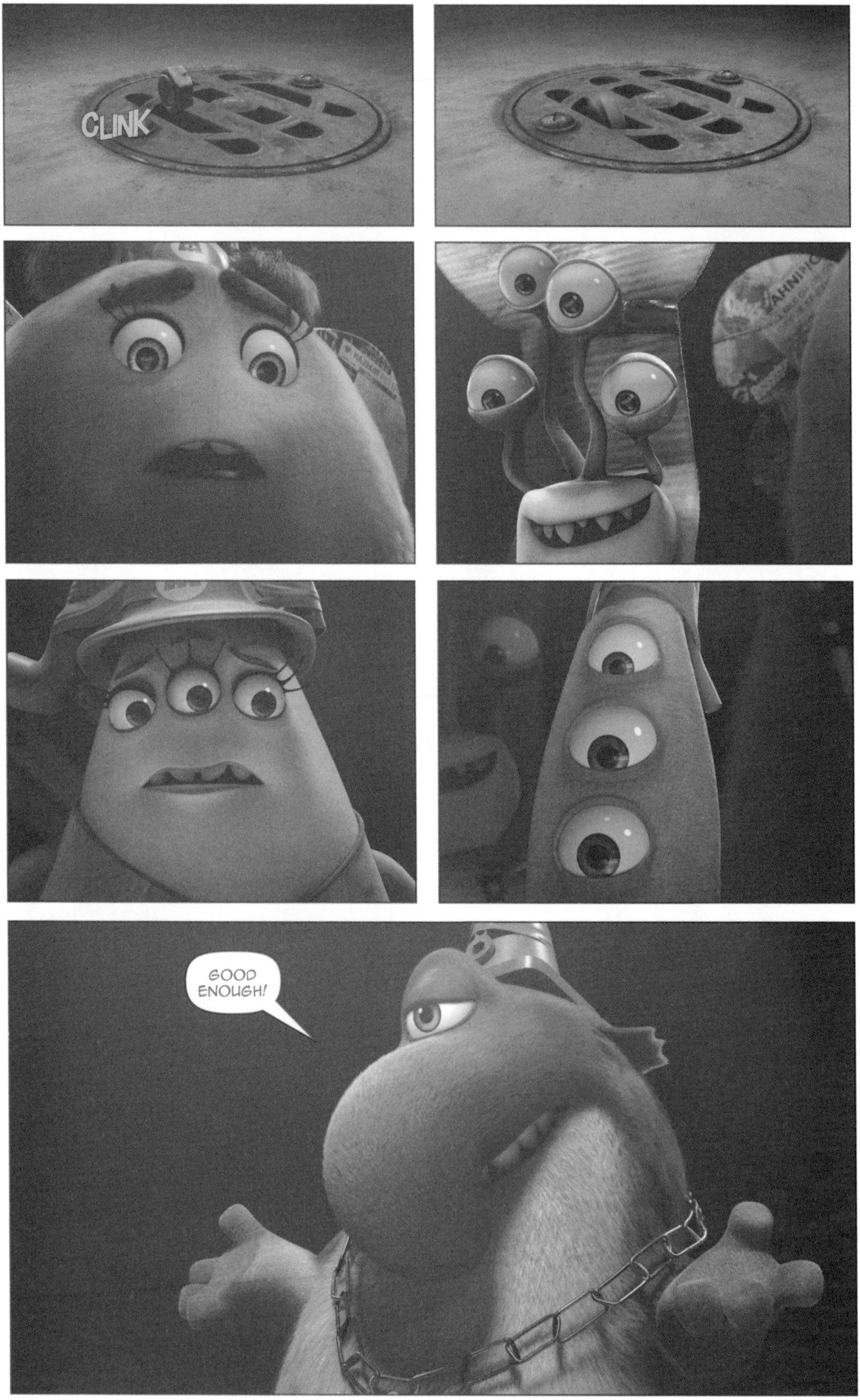
CLINK
GOOD ENOUGH!

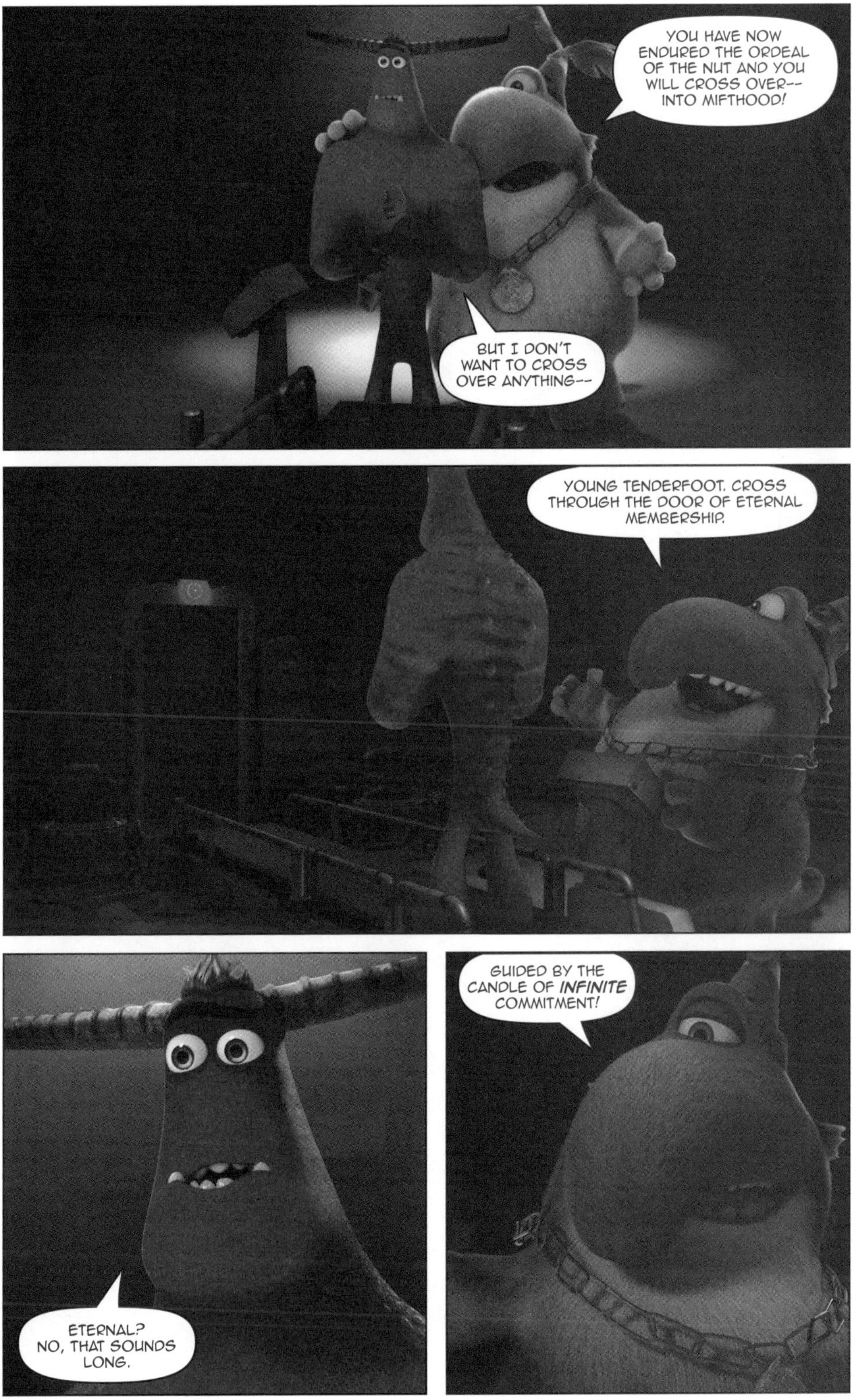
YOU HAVE NOW ENDURED THE ORDEAL OF THE NUT AND YOU WILL CROSS OVER-- INTO MIFTHOOD!
BUT I DON'T WANT TO CROSS OVER ANYTHING--
YOUNG TENDERFOOT. CROSS THROUGH THE DOOR OF ETERNAL MEMBERSHIP.
ETERNAL? NO, THAT SOUNDS LONG.
GUIDED BY THE CANDLE OF *INFINITE* COMMITMENT!

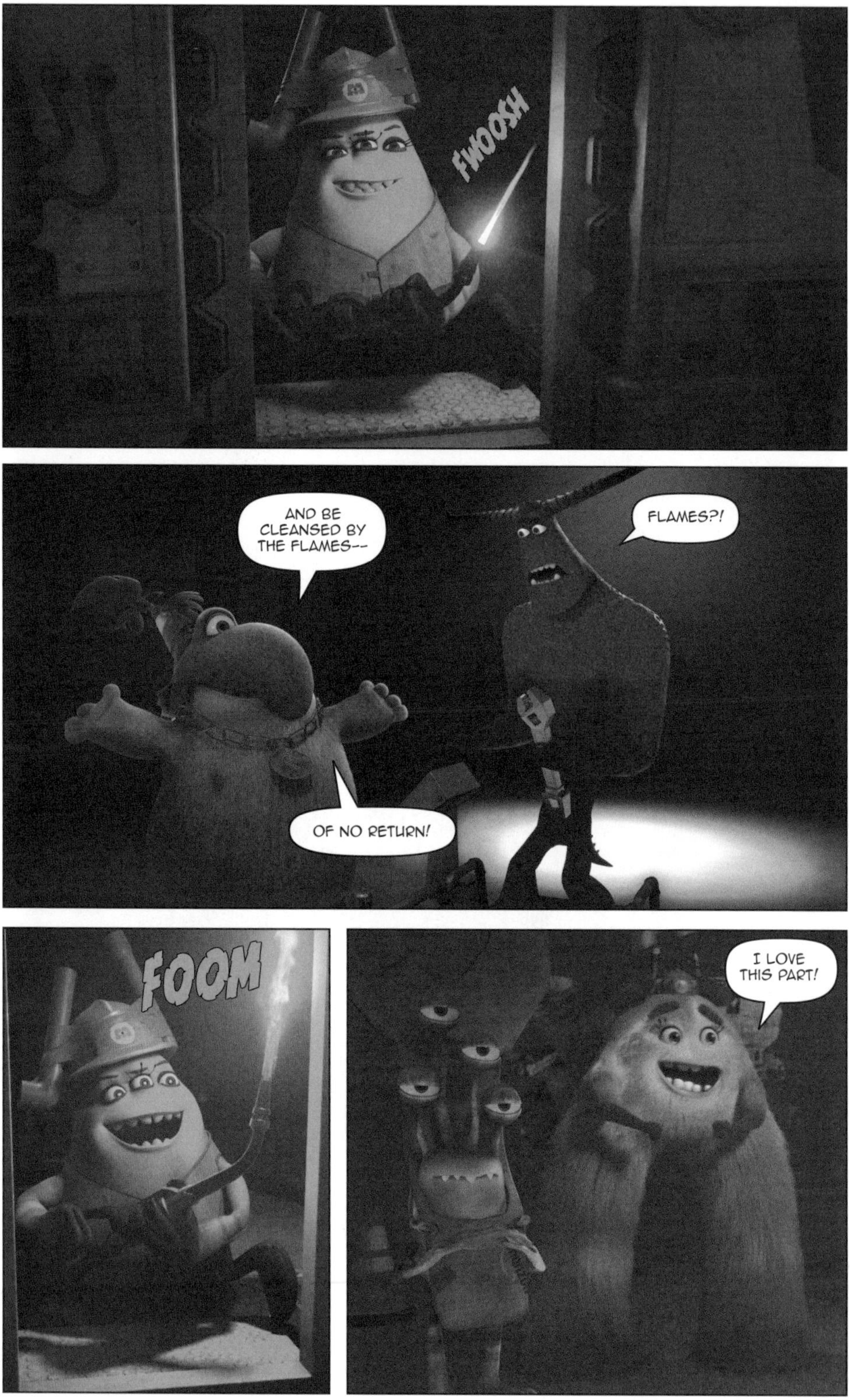
FWOOSH
AND BE CLEANSED BY THE FLAMES--
FLAMES?!
OF NO RETURN!
FOOM
I LOVE THIS PART!

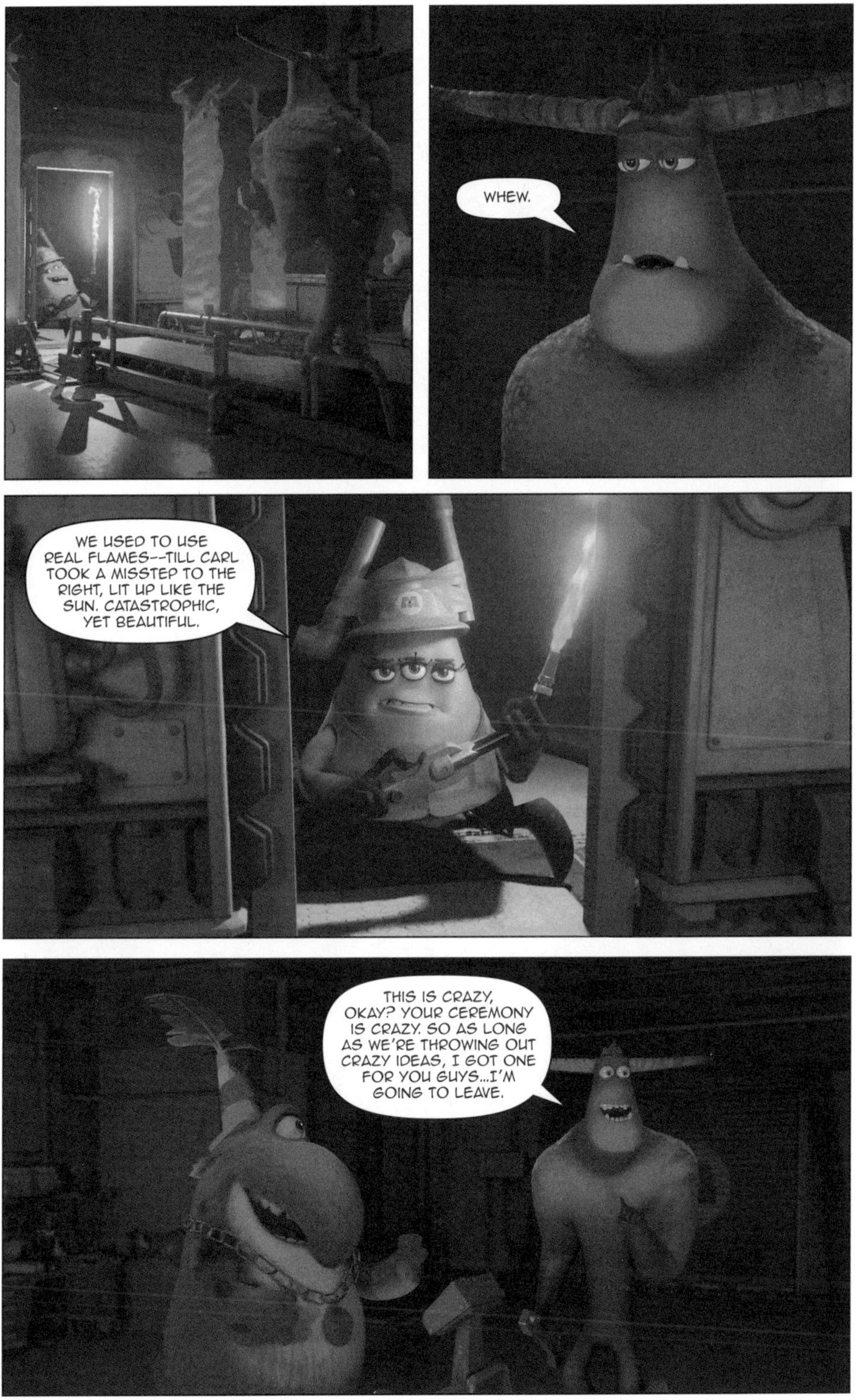
WHEW.
WE USED TO USE REAL FLAMES--TILL CARL TOOK A MISSTEP TO THE RIGHT, LIT UP LIKE THE SUN. CATASTROPHIC, YET BEAUTIFUL.
THIS IS CRAZY, OKAY? YOUR CEREMONY IS CRAZY. SO AS LONG AS WE'RE THROWING OUT CRAZY IDEAS, I GOT ONE FOR YOU GUYS...I'M GOING TO LEAVE.

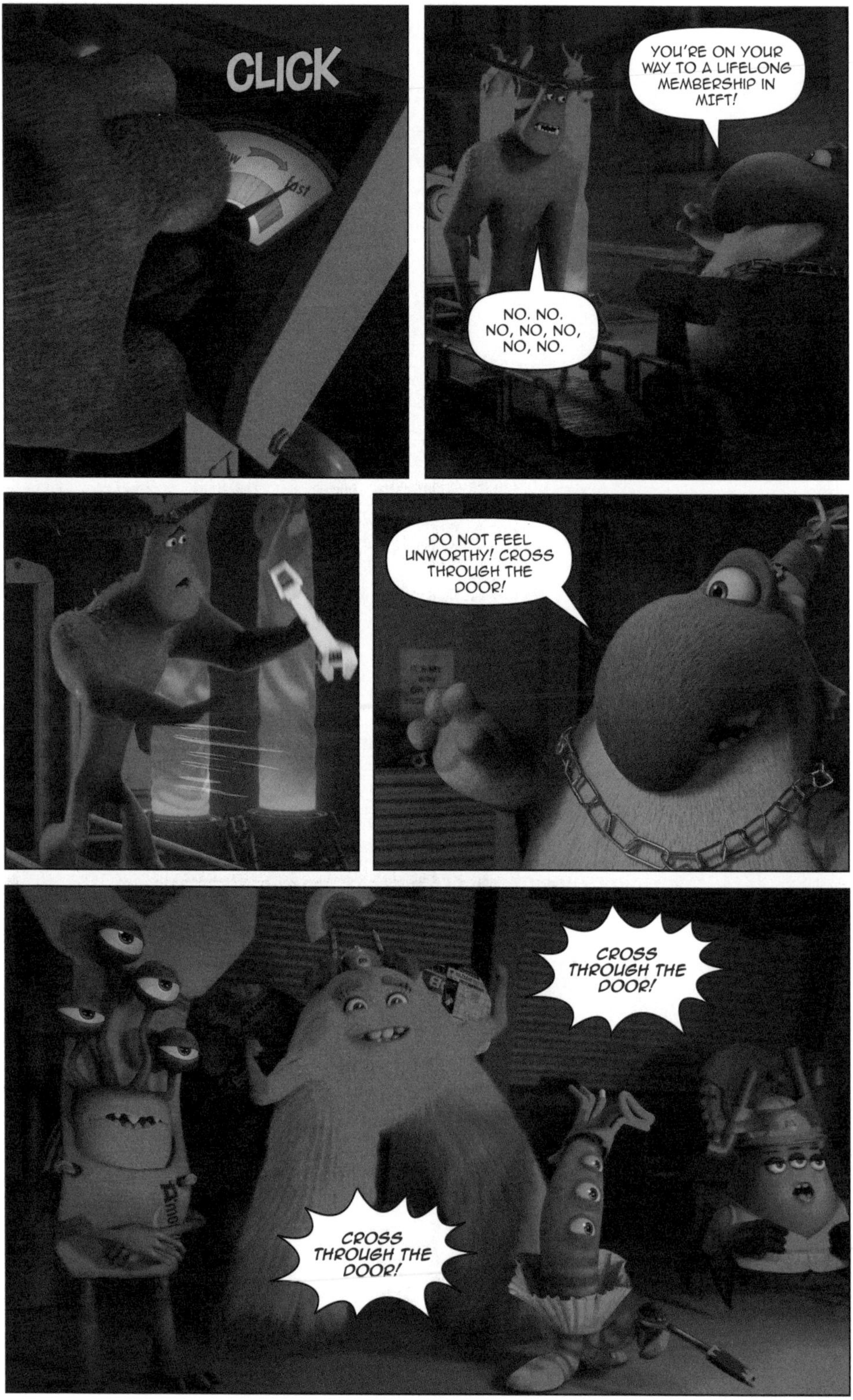
CLICK
fast
YOU'RE ON YOUR WAY TO A LIFELONG MEMBERSHIP IN MIFT!
NO. NO. NO, NO, NO, NO, NO.
DO NOT FEEL UNWORTHY! CROSS THROUGH THE DOOR!
CROSS THROUGH THE DOOR!
CROSS THROUGH THE DOOR!

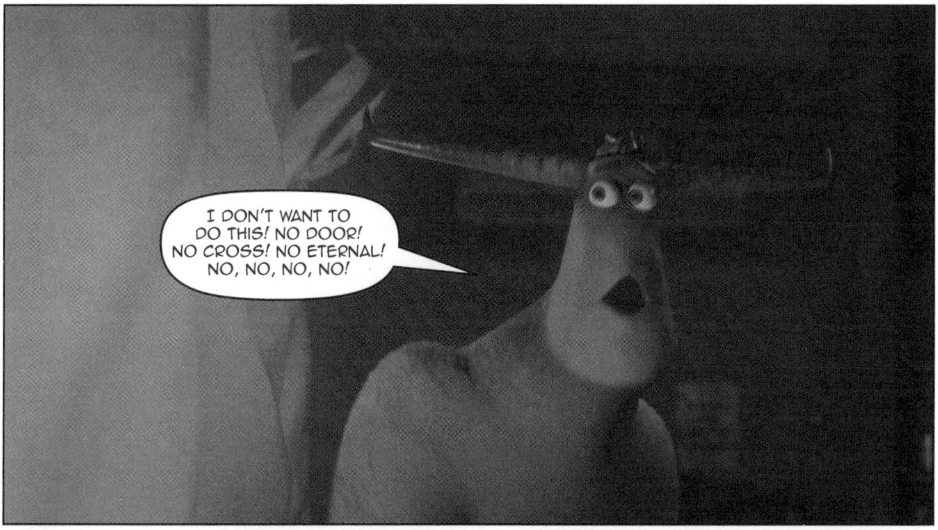
I DON'T WANT TO DO THIS! NO DOOR! NO CROSS! NO ETERNAL! NO, NO, NO, NO!

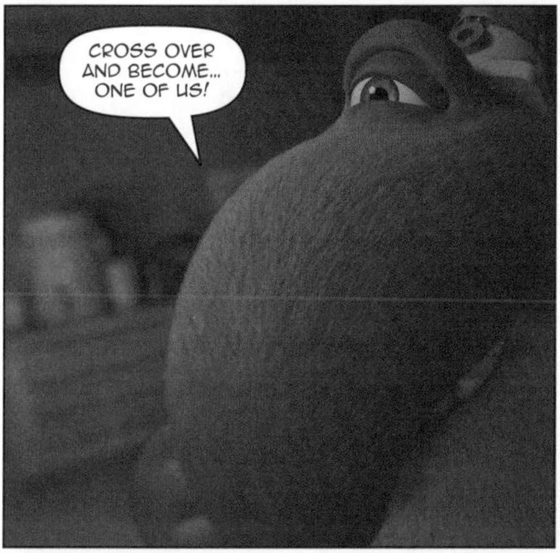
CROSS OVER AND BECOME... ONE OF US!

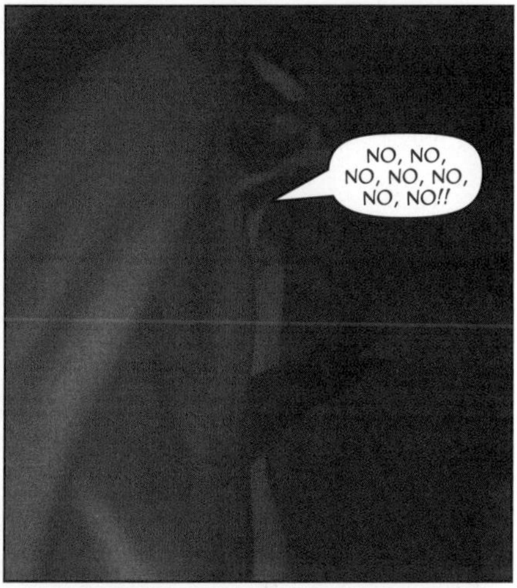
NO, NO, NO, NO, NO, NO, NO!!

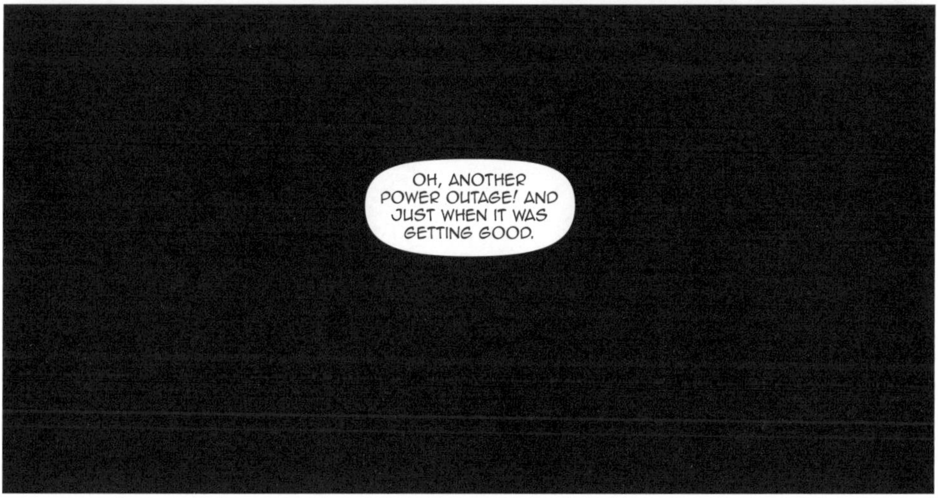
OH, ANOTHER POWER OUTAGE! AND JUST WHEN IT WAS GETTING GOOD.

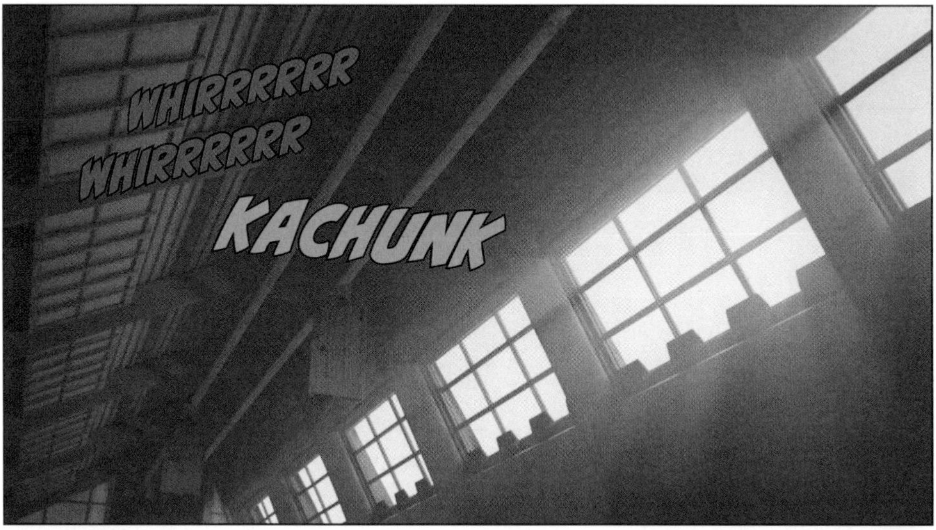
WHIRRRRRR
WHIRRRRRR
KACHUNK

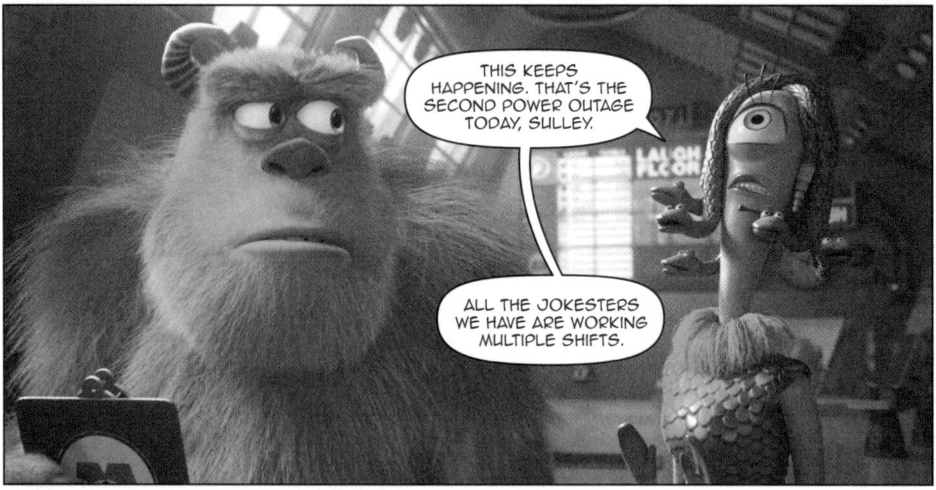
THIS KEEPS HAPPENING. THAT'S THE SECOND POWER OUTAGE TODAY, SULLEY.
ALL THE JOKESTERS WE HAVE ARE WORKING MULTIPLE SHIFTS.

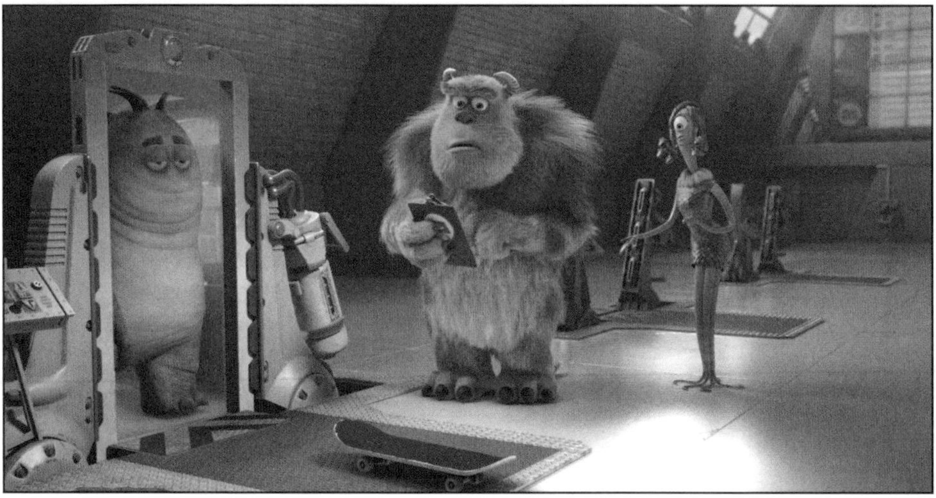

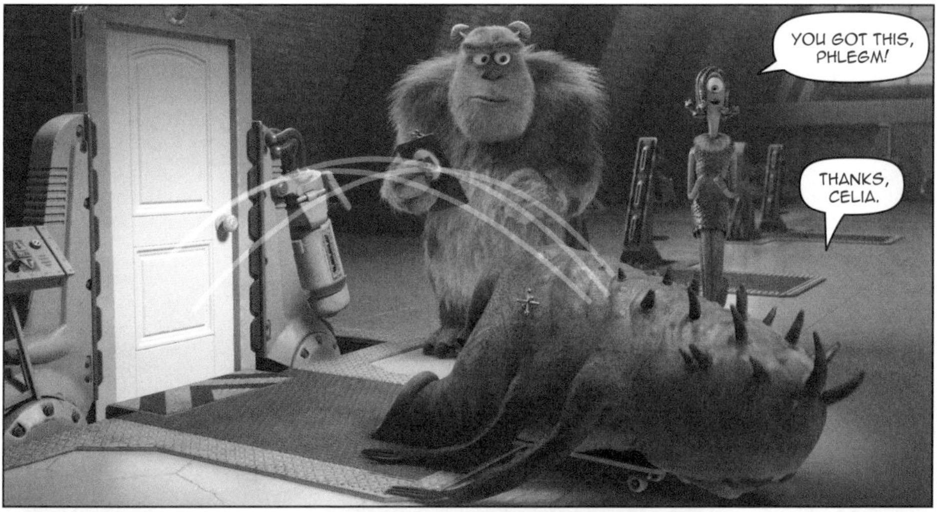
YOU GOT THIS, PHLEGM!
THANKS, CELIA.

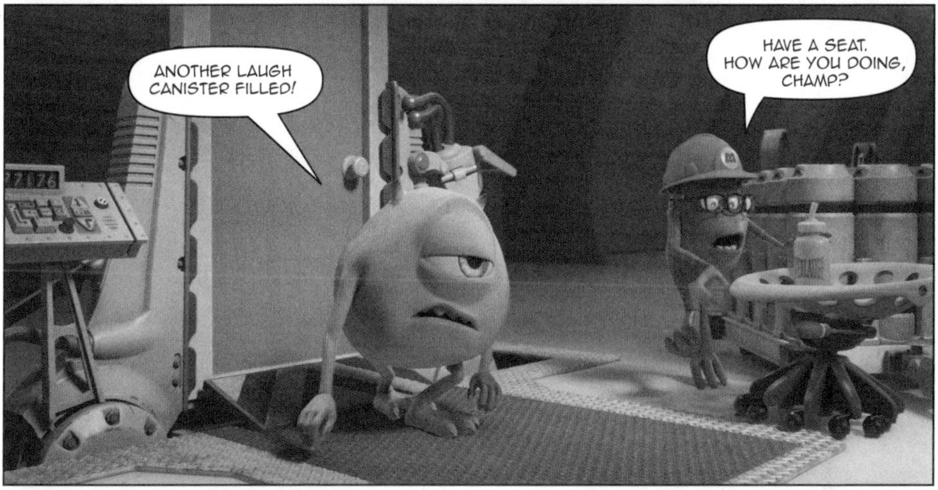
ANOTHER LAUGH CANISTER FILLED!
HAVE A SEAT. HOW ARE YOU DOING, CHAMP?

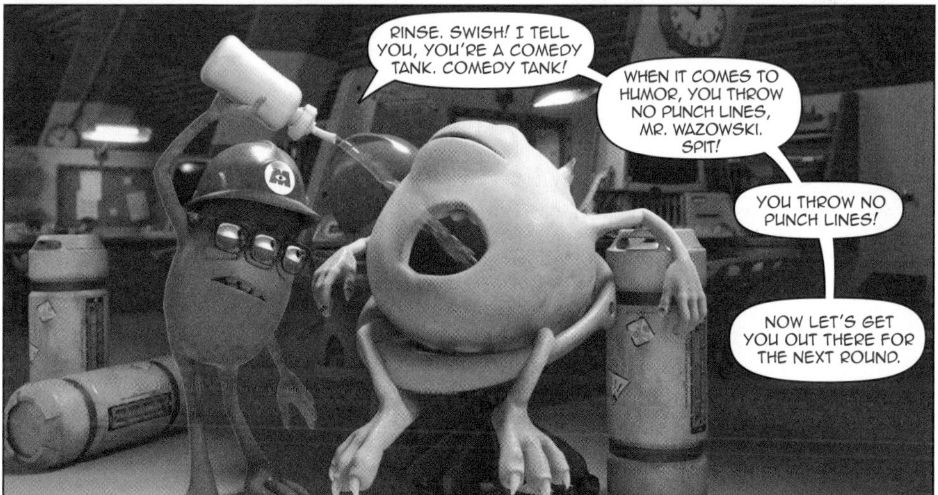
RINSE. SWISH! I TELL YOU, YOU'RE A COMEDY TANK. COMEDY TANK!
WHEN IT COMES TO HUMOR, YOU THROW NO PUNCH LINES, MR. WAZOWSKI. SPIT!
YOU THROW NO PUNCH LINES!
NOW LET'S GET YOU OUT THERE FOR THE NEXT ROUND.

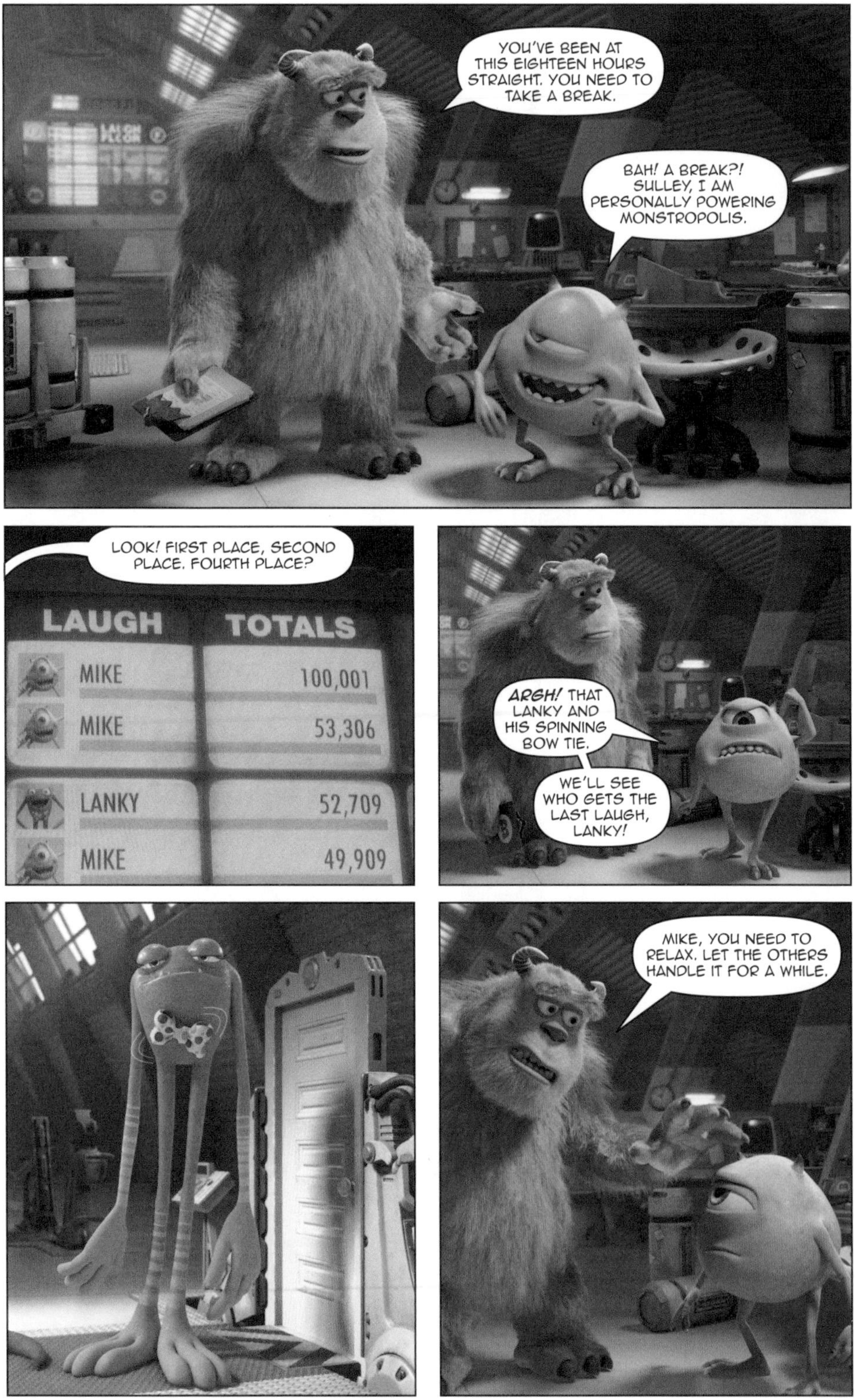
YOU'VE BEEN AT THIS EIGHTEEN HOURS STRAIGHT. YOU NEED TO TAKE A BREAK.
BAH! A BREAK?! SULLEY, I AM PERSONALLY POWERING MONSTROPOLIS.
LOOK! FIRST PLACE, SECOND PLACE. FOURTH PLACE?
LAUGH TOTALS
MIKE 100,001
MIKE 53,306
LANKY 52,709
MIKE 49,909
ARGH! THAT LANKY AND HIS SPINNING BOW TIE.
WE'LL SEE WHO GETS THE LAST LAUGH, LANKY!
MIKE, YOU NEED TO RELAX. LET THE OTHERS HANDLE IT FOR A WHILE.

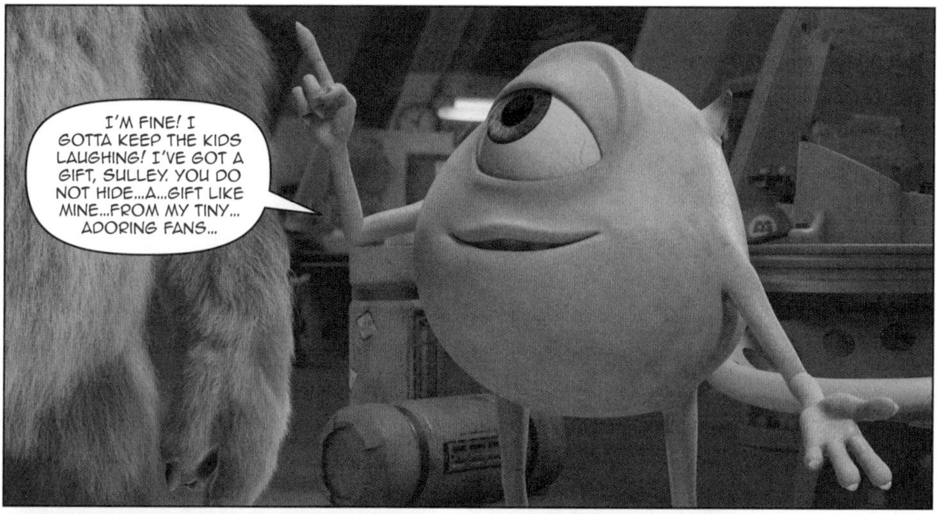
I'M FINE! I GOTTA KEEP THE KIDS LAUGHING! I'VE GOT A GIFT, SULLEY. YOU DO NOT HIDE...A...GIFT LIKE MINE...FROM MY TINY... ADORING FANS...

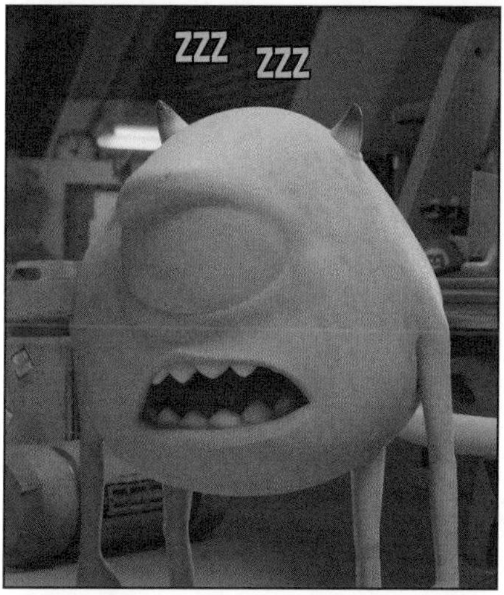
ZZZ
ZZZ

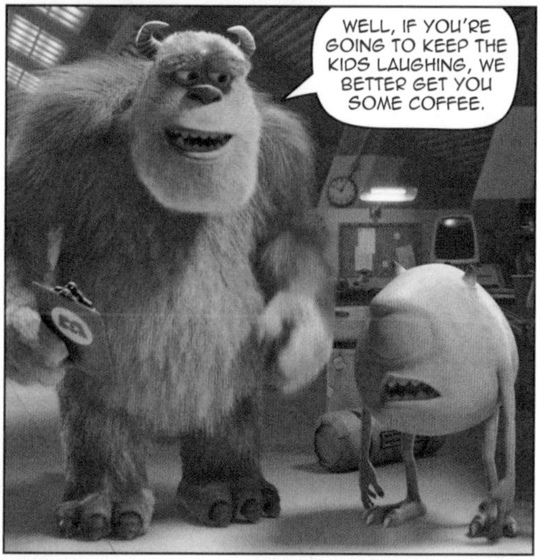
WELL, IF YOU'RE GOING TO KEEP THE KIDS LAUGHING, WE BETTER GET YOU SOME COFFEE.

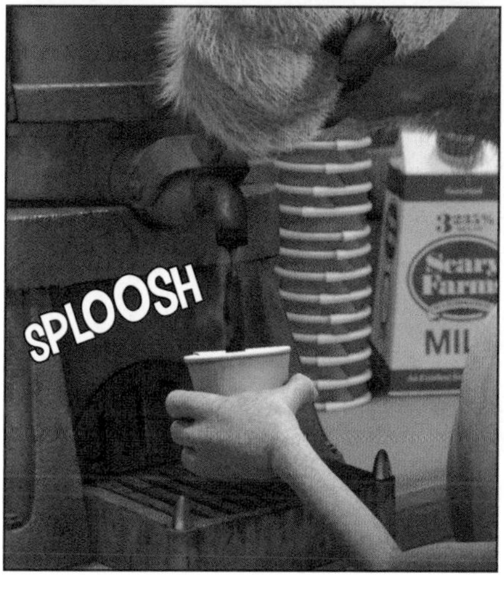
SPLOOSH

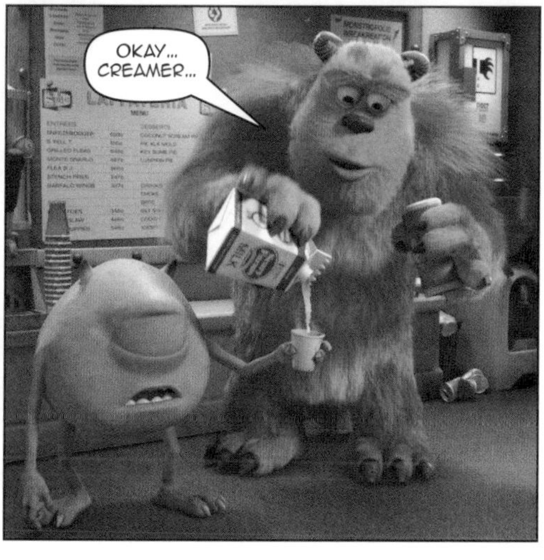
OKAY... CREAMER...

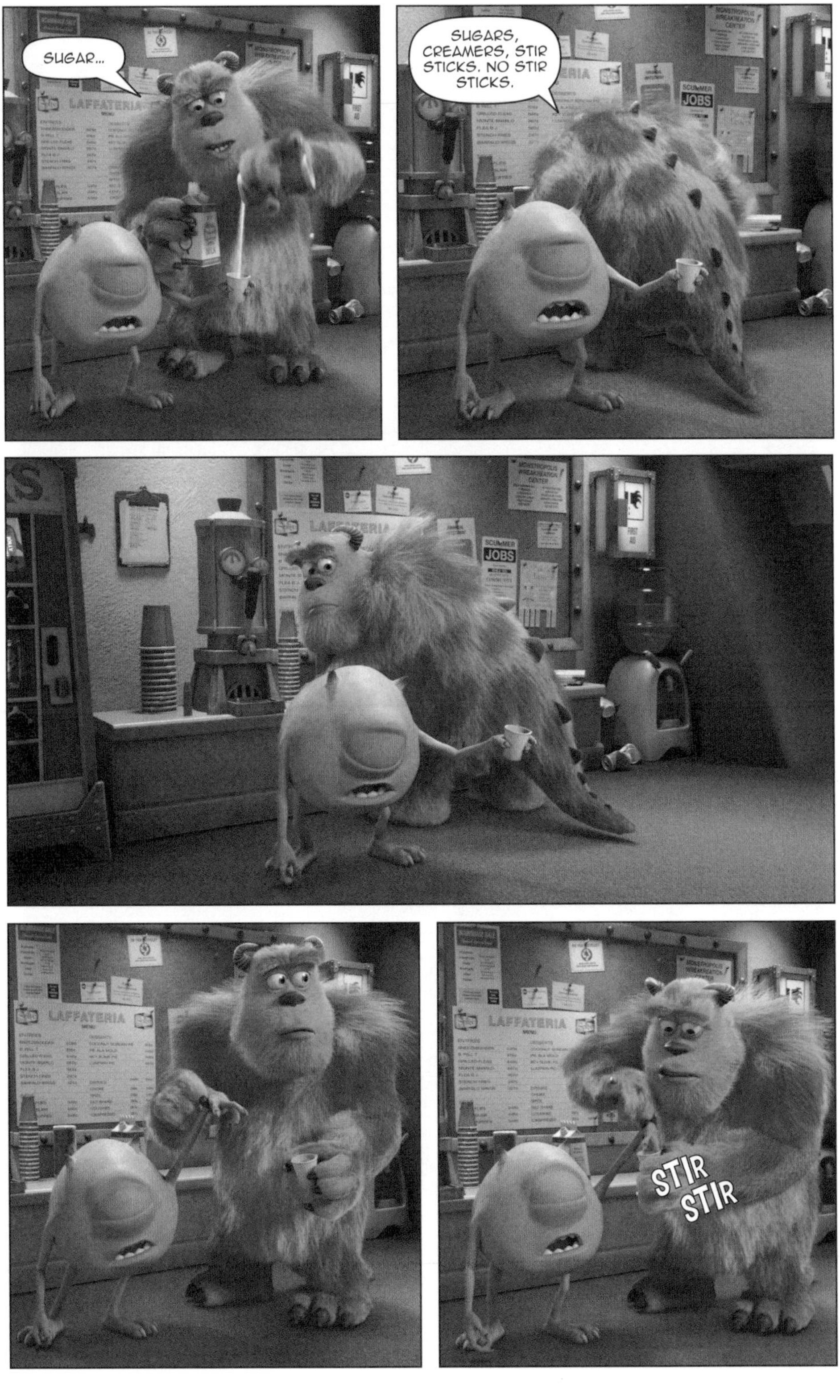
SUGAR...
SUGARS, CREAMERS, STIR STICKS. NO STIR STICKS.
STIR
STIR

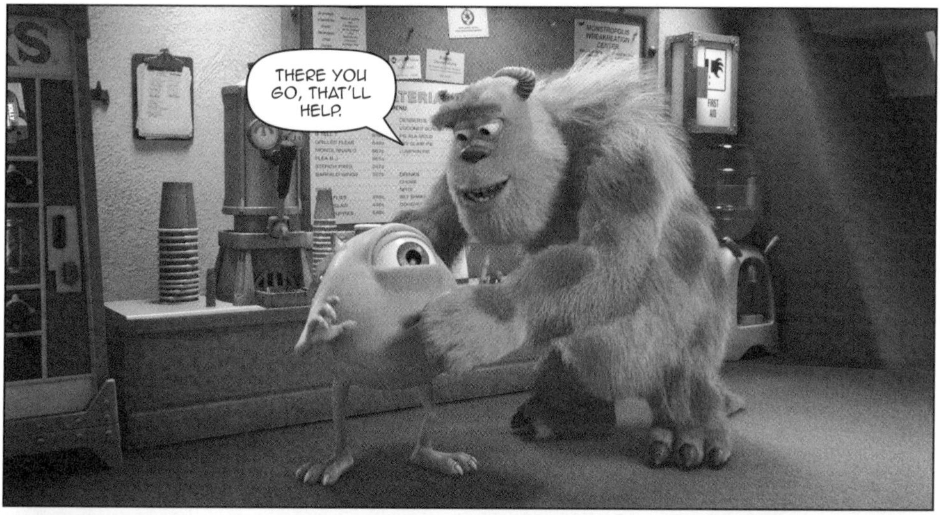
THERE YOU GO, THAT'LL HELP.

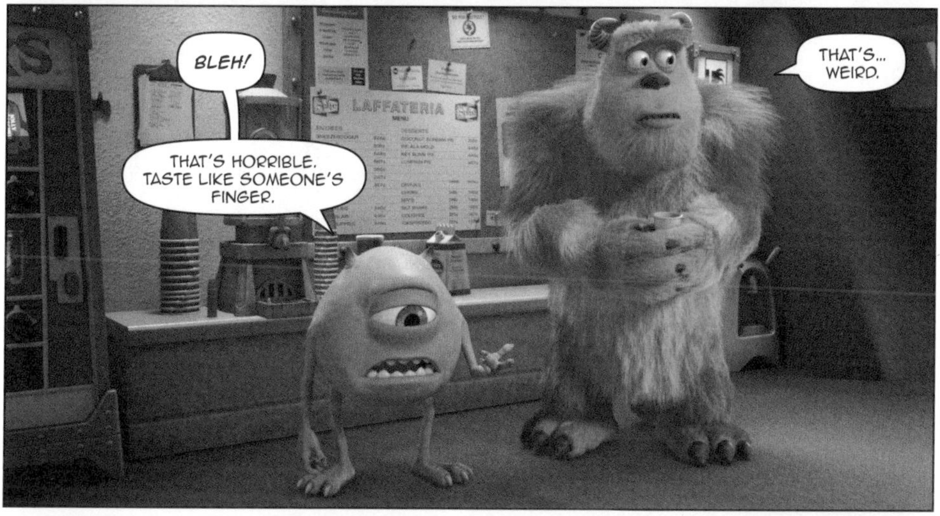
BLEH!
THAT'S HORRIBLE. TASTE LIKE SOMEONE'S FINGER.
THAT'S... WEIRD.

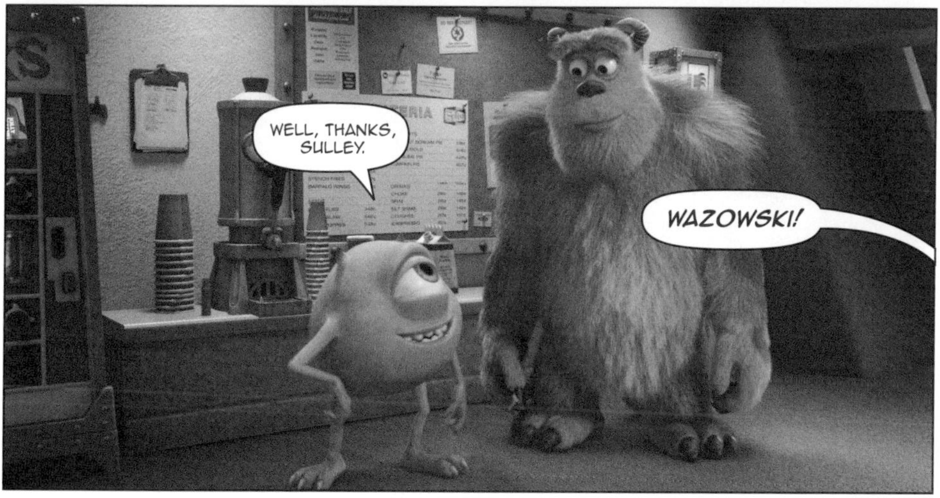
WELL, THANKS, SULLEY.
WAZOWSKI!

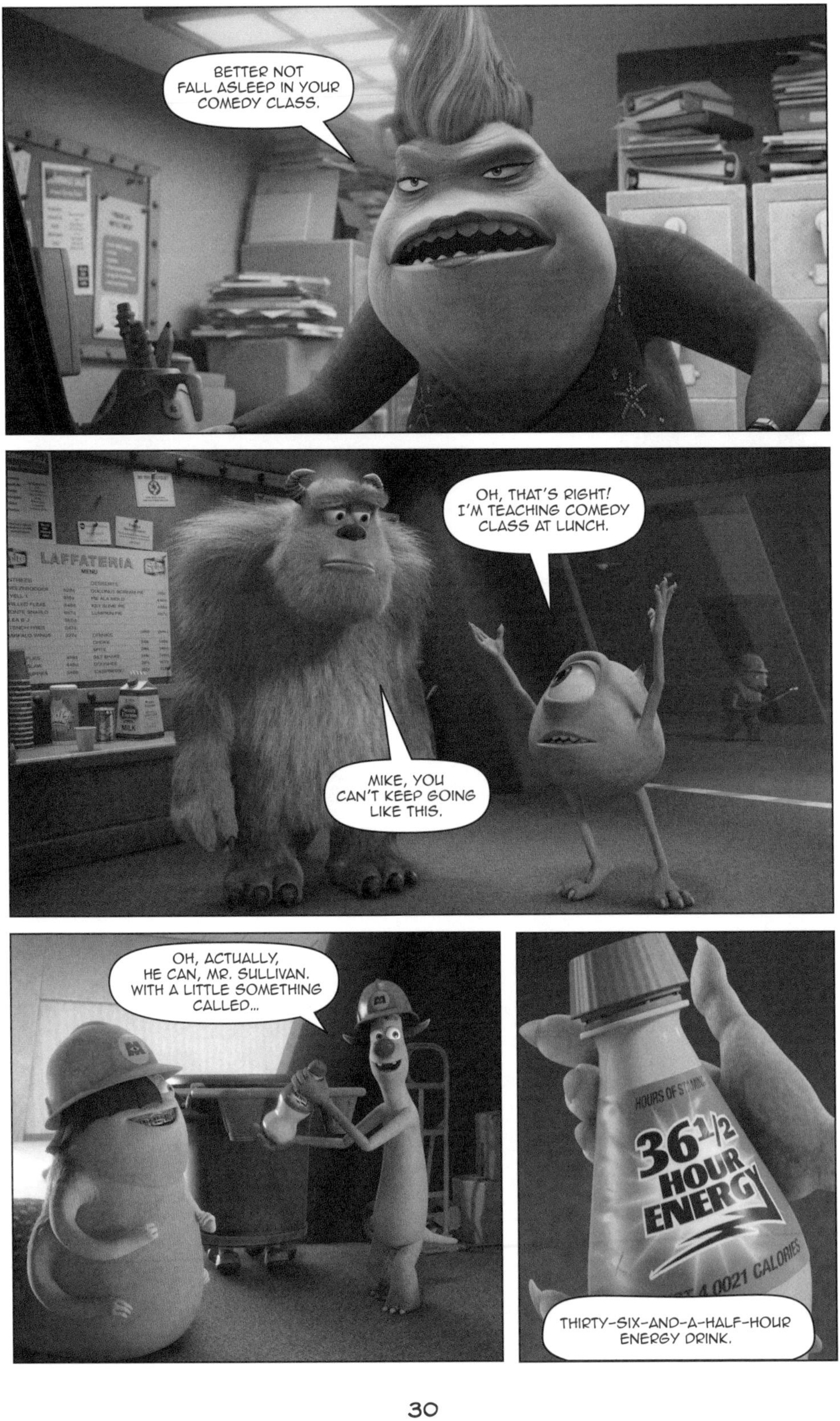
BETTER NOT FALL ASLEEP IN YOUR COMEDY CLASS.
LAFFATERIA
MENU
OH, THAT'S RIGHT! I'M TEACHING COMEDY CLASS AT LUNCH.
MIKE, YOU CAN'T KEEP GOING LIKE THIS.
OH, ACTUALLY, HE CAN, MR. SULLIVAN. WITH A LITTLE SOMETHING CALLED...
36 1/2 HOUR ENERGY
THIRTY-SIX-AND-A-HALF-HOUR ENERGY DRINK.

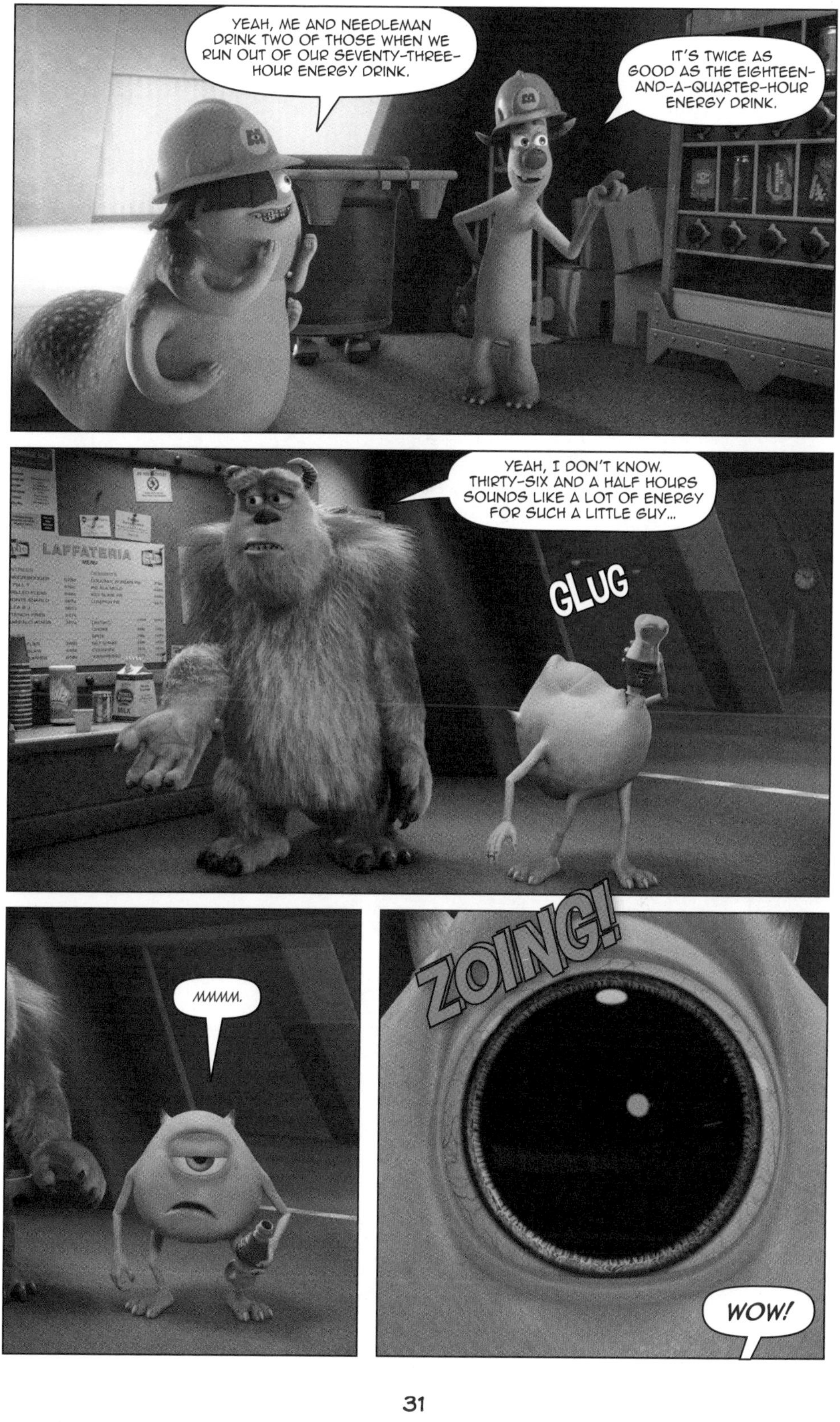
YEAH, ME AND NEEDLEMAN DRINK TWO OF THOSE WHEN WE RUN OUT OF OUR SEVENTY-THREE-HOUR ENERGY DRINK.
IT'S TWICE AS GOOD AS THE EIGHTEEN-AND-A-QUARTER-HOUR ENERGY DRINK.
YEAH, I DON'T KNOW. THIRTY-SIX AND A HALF HOURS SOUNDS LIKE A LOT OF ENERGY FOR SUCH A LITTLE GUY...
GLUG
LAFFATERIA
MILK
MMMM.
ZOING!
WOW!

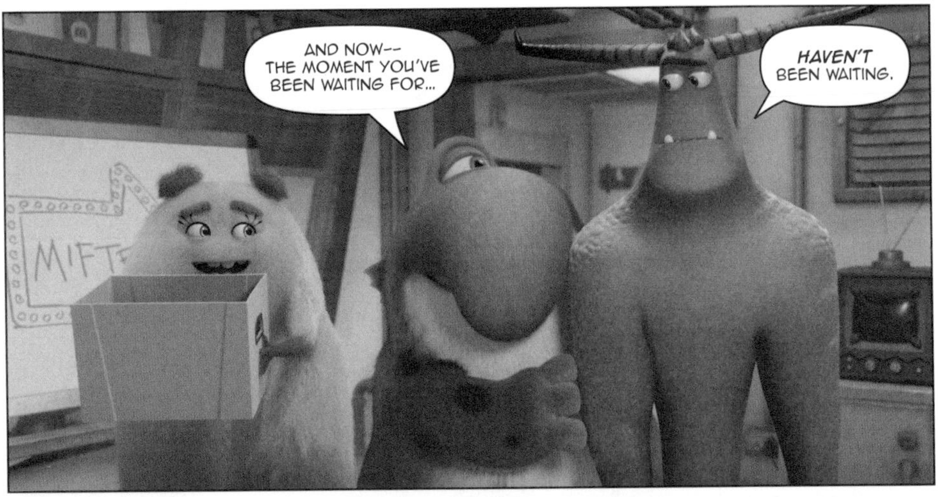
AND NOW--
THE MOMENT YOU'VE
BEEN WAITING FOR...
HAVEN'T
BEEN WAITING.

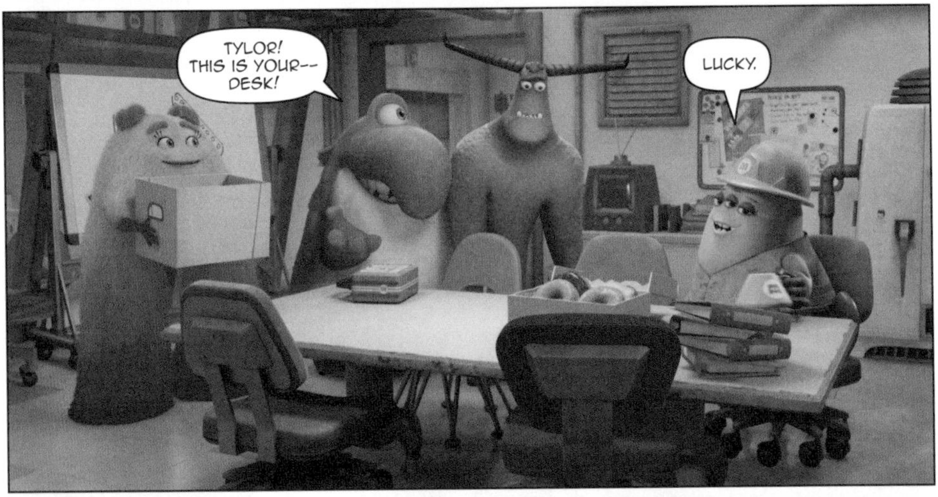
TYLOR!
THIS IS YOUR--
DESK!
LUCKY.

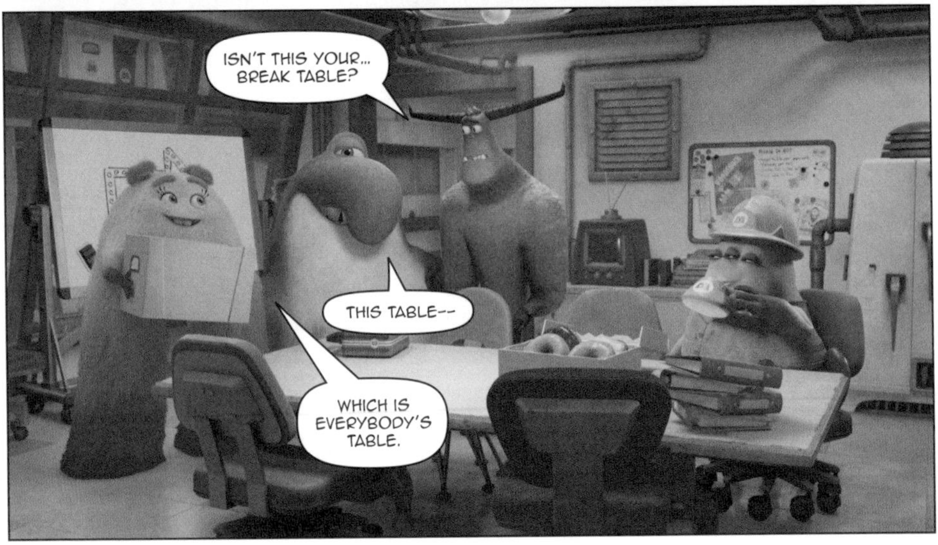
ISN'T THIS YOUR...
BREAK TABLE?
THIS TABLE--
WHICH IS
EVERYBODY'S
TABLE.

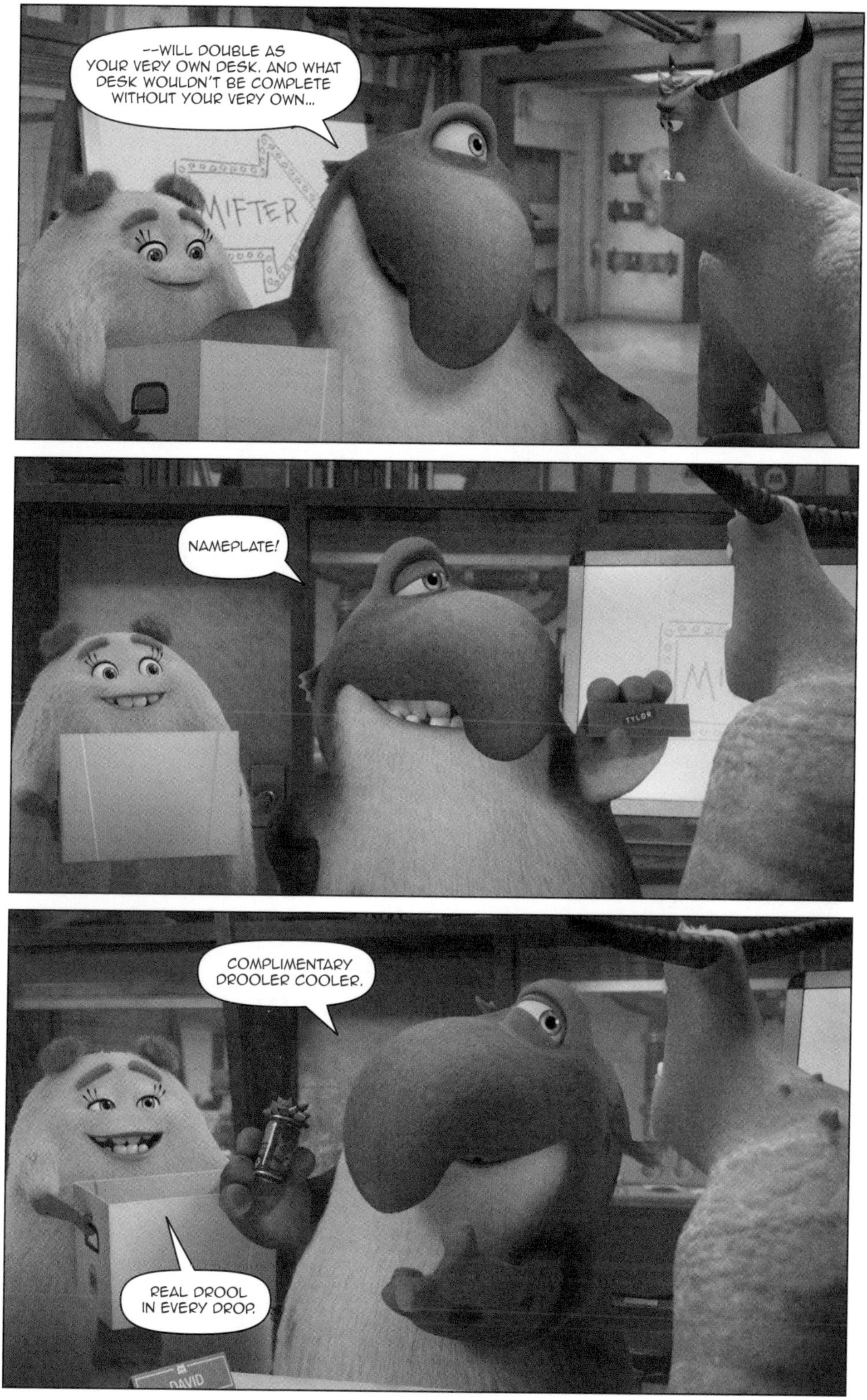
--WILL DOUBLE AS YOUR VERY OWN DESK. AND WHAT DESK WOULDN'T BE COMPLETE WITHOUT YOUR VERY OWN...
NAMEPLATE!
COMPLIMENTARY DROOLER COOLER.
REAL DROOL IN EVERY DROP.

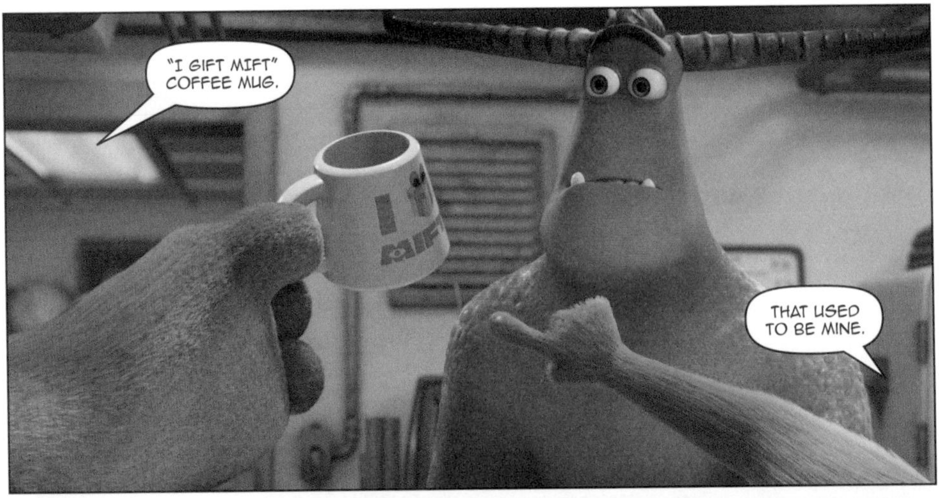
"I GIFT MIFT" COFFEE MUG.
THAT USED TO BE MINE.

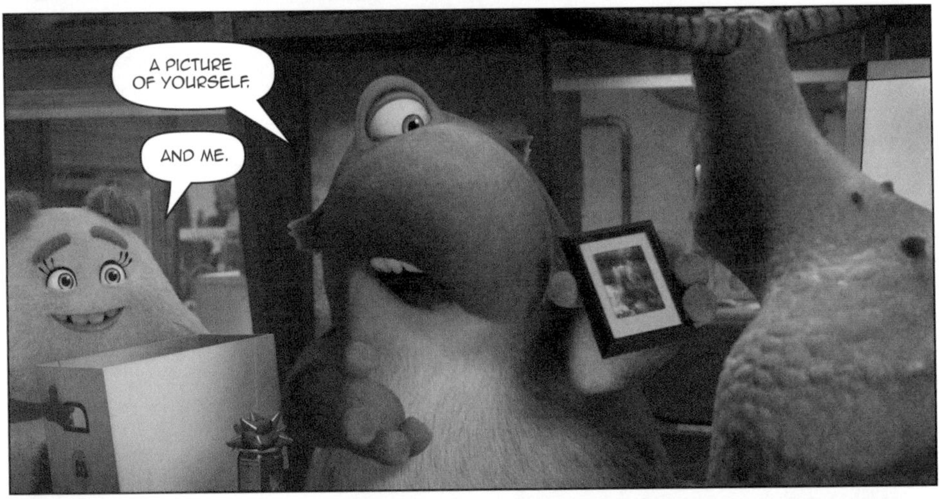
A PICTURE OF YOURSELF.
AND ME.

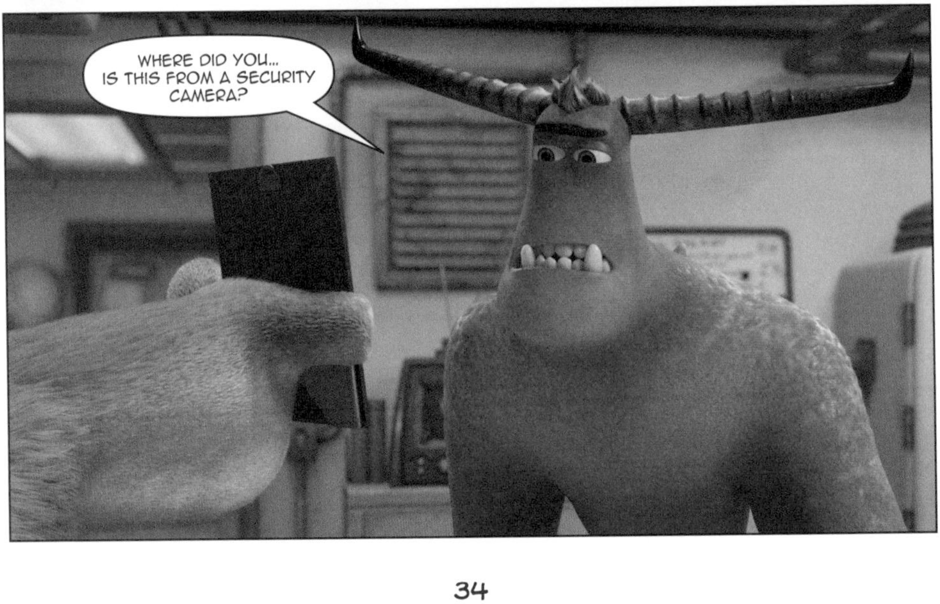
WHERE DID YOU... IS THIS FROM A SECURITY CAMERA?

AND LAST BUT NOT LEAST--

YOUR CEREMONIAL SACRED WRENCH. ENGRAVED...

I ENGRAVED IT MYSELF.

WITH THE NAME OF OUR NEWEST MEMBER.

WELCOME, TYLOR.

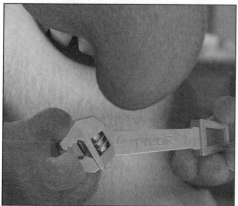

WOW. I MEAN, YOU REALLY SHOULDN'T HAVE GONE TO ALL THIS TROUBLE.

I AM NOT GOING TO BE HERE THAT LONG.

OH, I LIKE THE SOUND OF THAT. DO YOU LIKE IT, ROTO?

ROTO DOESN'T TRUST IT. THEREFORE, I DON'T TRUST IT.

GRRRWWL

DUNCAN

IN

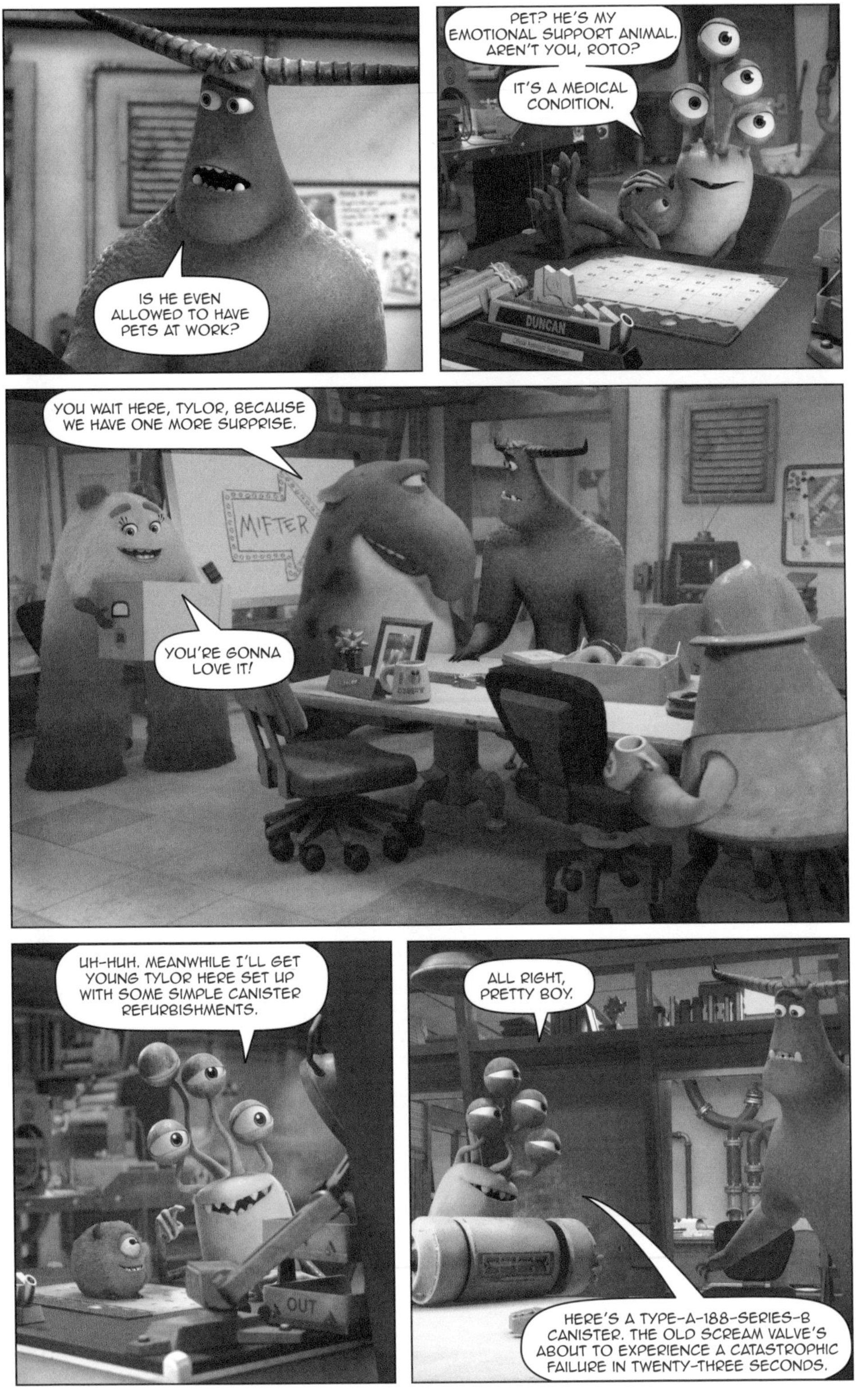
IS HE EVEN ALLOWED TO HAVE PETS AT WORK?
PET? HE'S MY EMOTIONAL SUPPORT ANIMAL. AREN'T YOU, ROTO?
IT'S A MEDICAL CONDITION.
DUNCAN
YOU WAIT HERE, TYLOR, BECAUSE WE HAVE ONE MORE SURPRISE.
MIFTER
YOU'RE GONNA LOVE IT!
UH-HUH. MEANWHILE I'LL GET YOUNG TYLOR HERE SET UP WITH SOME SIMPLE CANISTER REFURBISHMENTS.
OUT
ALL RIGHT, PRETTY BOY.
HERE'S A TYPE-A-188-SERIES-B CANISTER. THE OLD SCREAM VALVE'S ABOUT TO EXPERIENCE A CATASTROPHIC FAILURE IN TWENTY-THREE SECONDS.

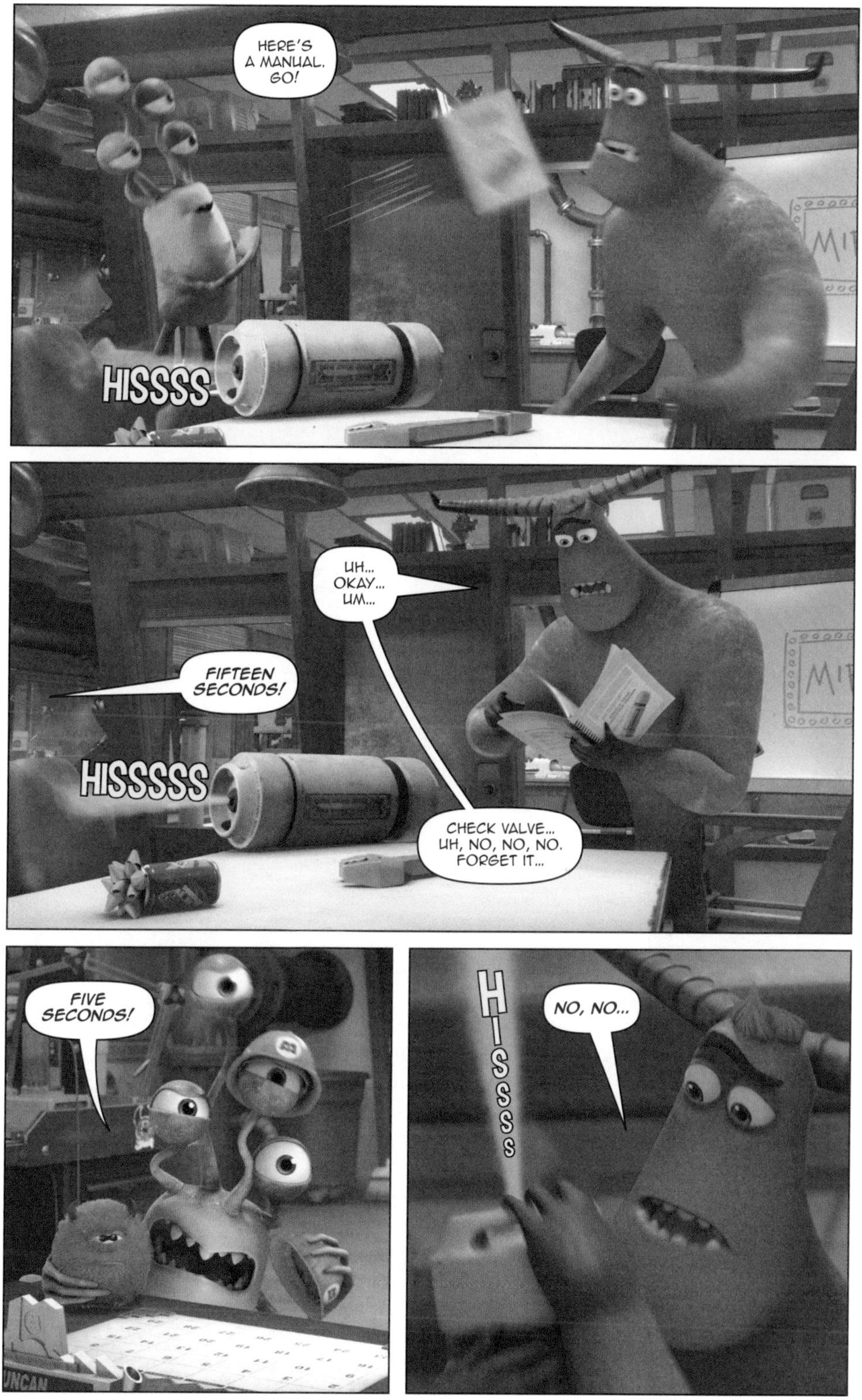
HERE'S A MANUAL. GO!
HISSSS
UH... OKAY... UM...
FIFTEEN SECONDS!
HISSSSS
CHECK VALVE... UH, NO, NO, NO. FORGET IT...
FIVE SECONDS!
HISSSS
NO, NO...

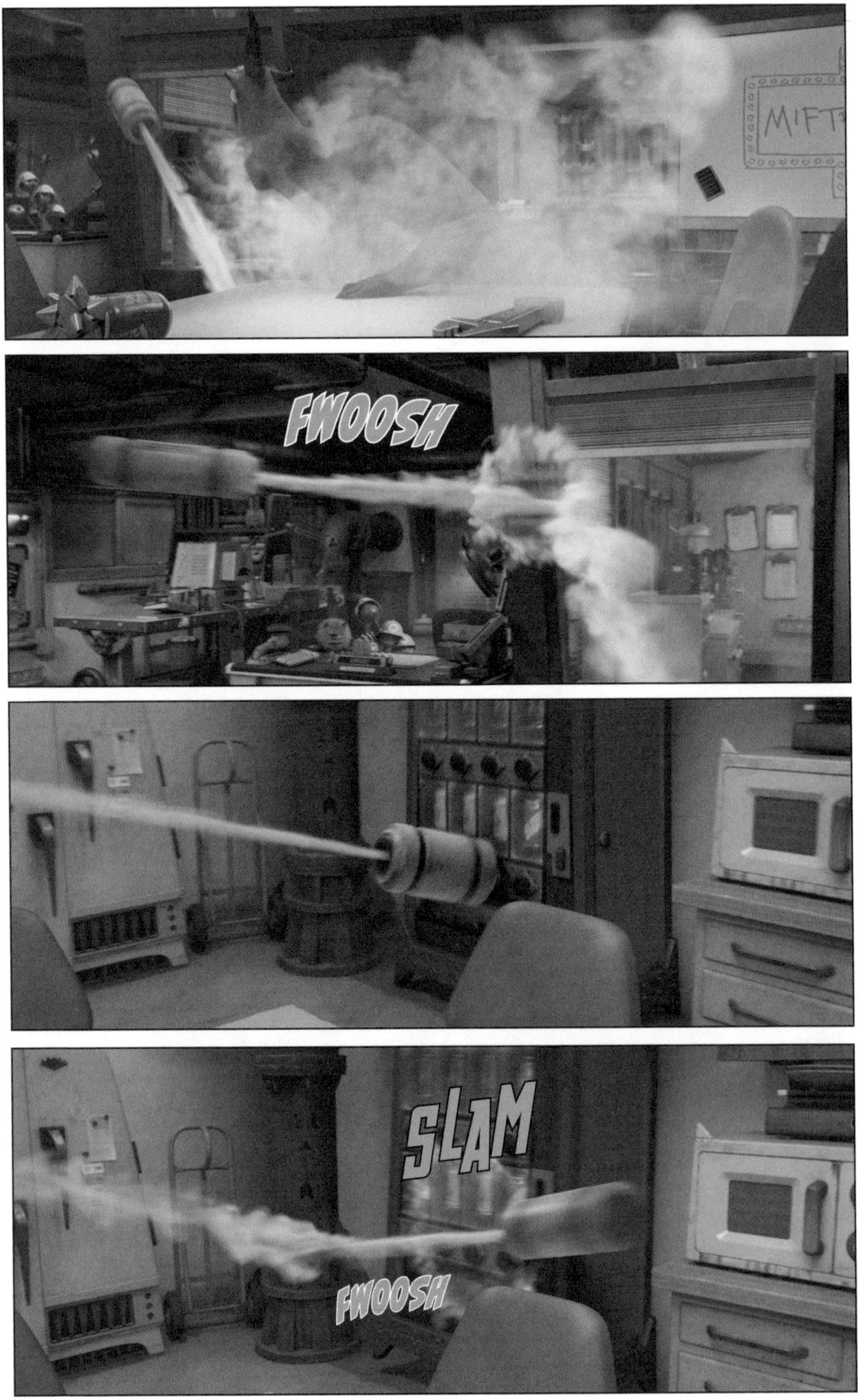
FWOOSH
SLAM
FWOOSH

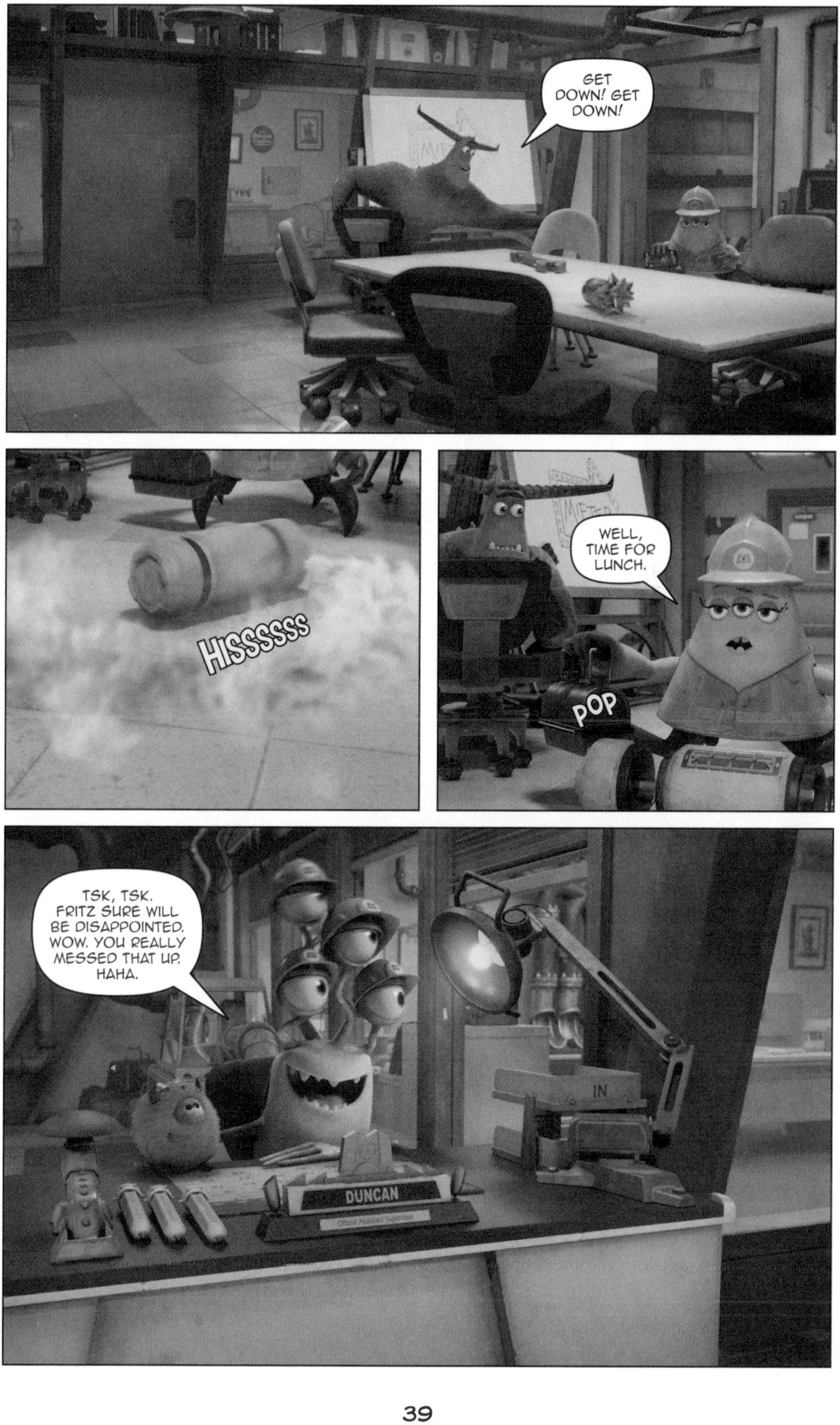
GET DOWN! GET DOWN!
HISSSSSS
WELL, TIME FOR LUNCH.
POP
TSK, TSK. FRITZ SURE WILL BE DISAPPOINTED. WOW. YOU REALLY MESSED THAT UP. HAHA.
IN
DUNCAN

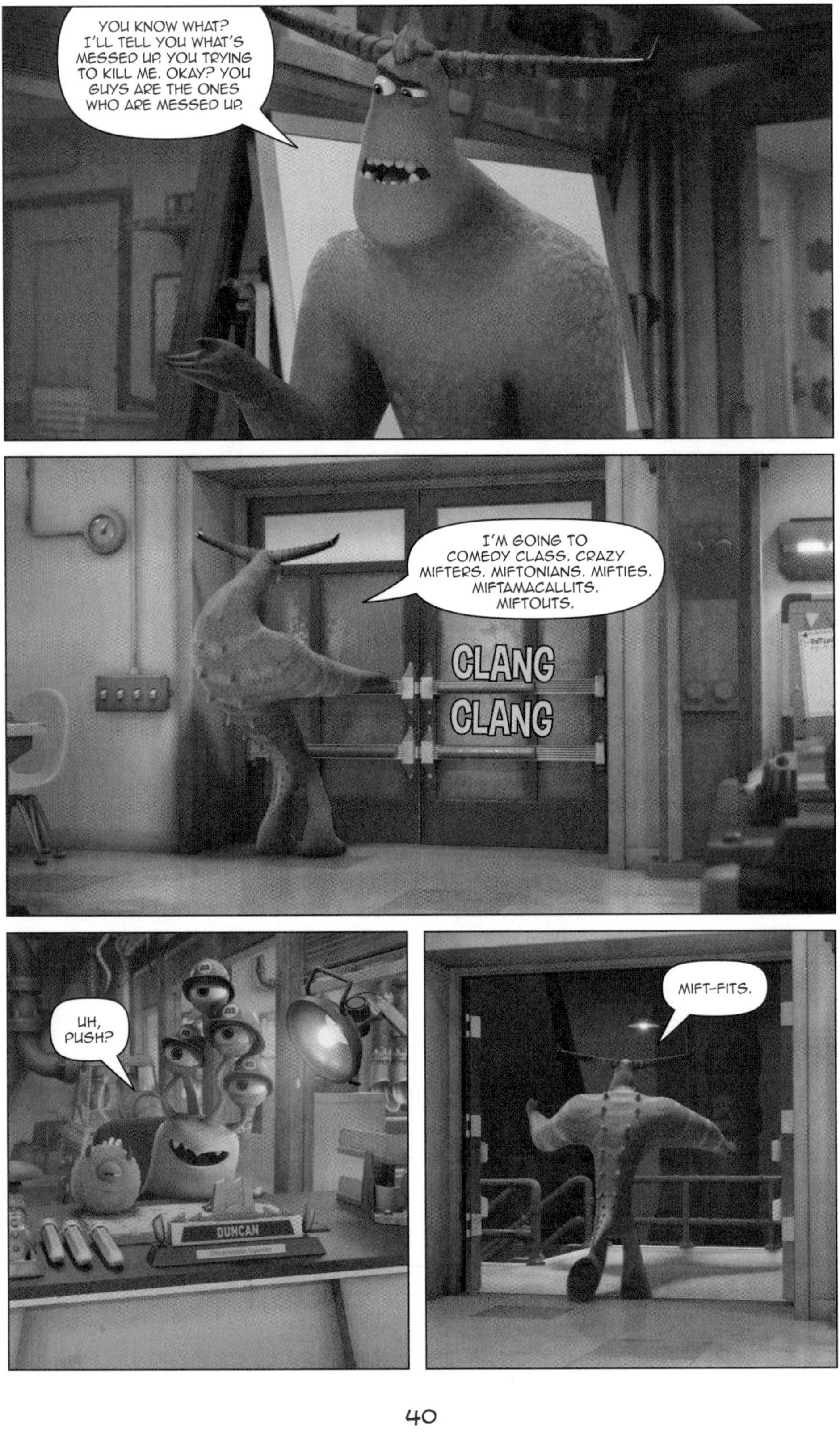
YOU KNOW WHAT? I'LL TELL YOU WHAT'S MESSED UP. YOU TRYING TO KILL ME. OKAY? YOU GUYS ARE THE ONES WHO ARE MESSED UP.
I'M GOING TO COMEDY CLASS. CRAZY MIFTERS. MIFTONIANS. MIFTIES. MIFTAMACALLITS. MIFTOUTS.
CLANG
CLANG
UH, PUSH?
DUNCAN
MIFT-FITS.

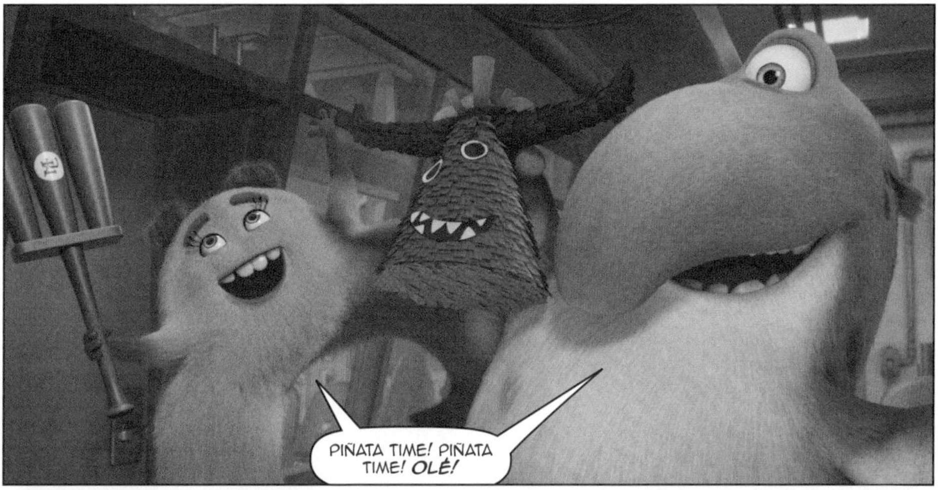
PIÑATA TIME! PIÑATA TIME! OLÉ!

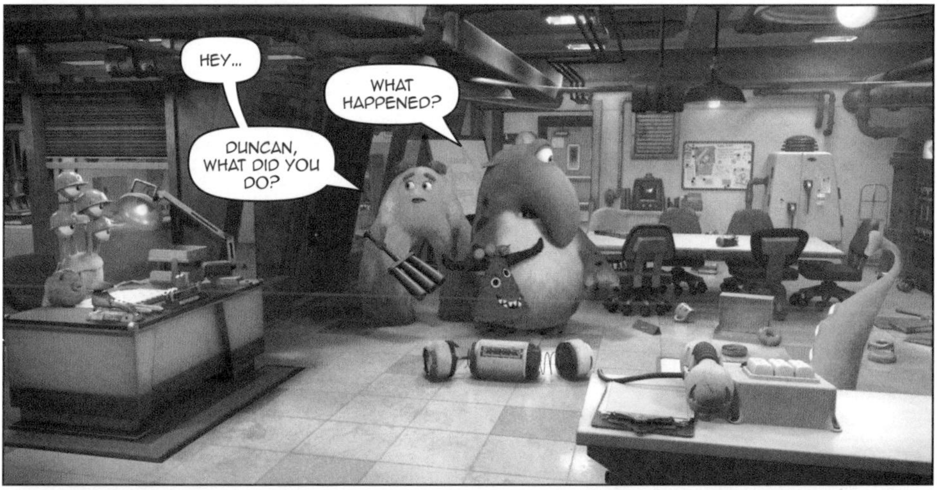
HEY...
WHAT HAPPENED?
DUNCAN, WHAT DID YOU DO?

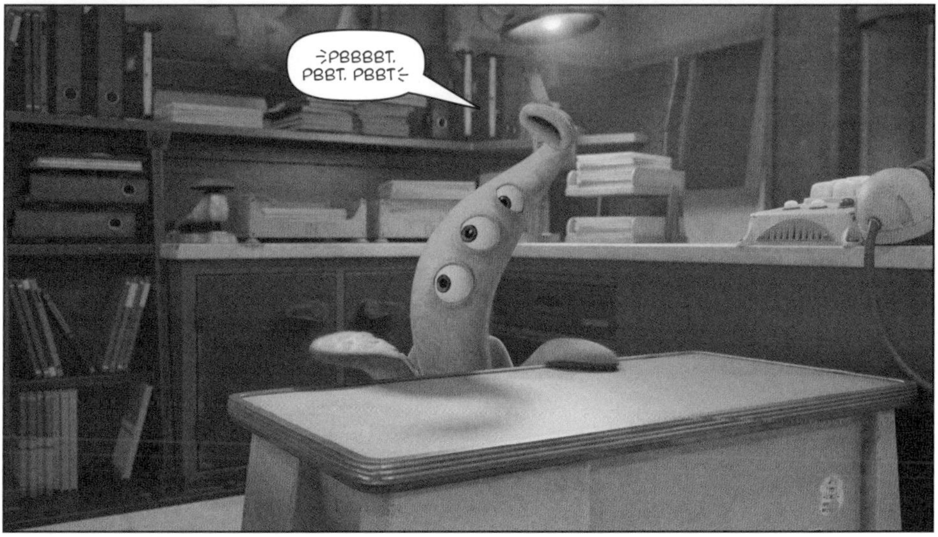
PBBBBT. PBBT. PBBT

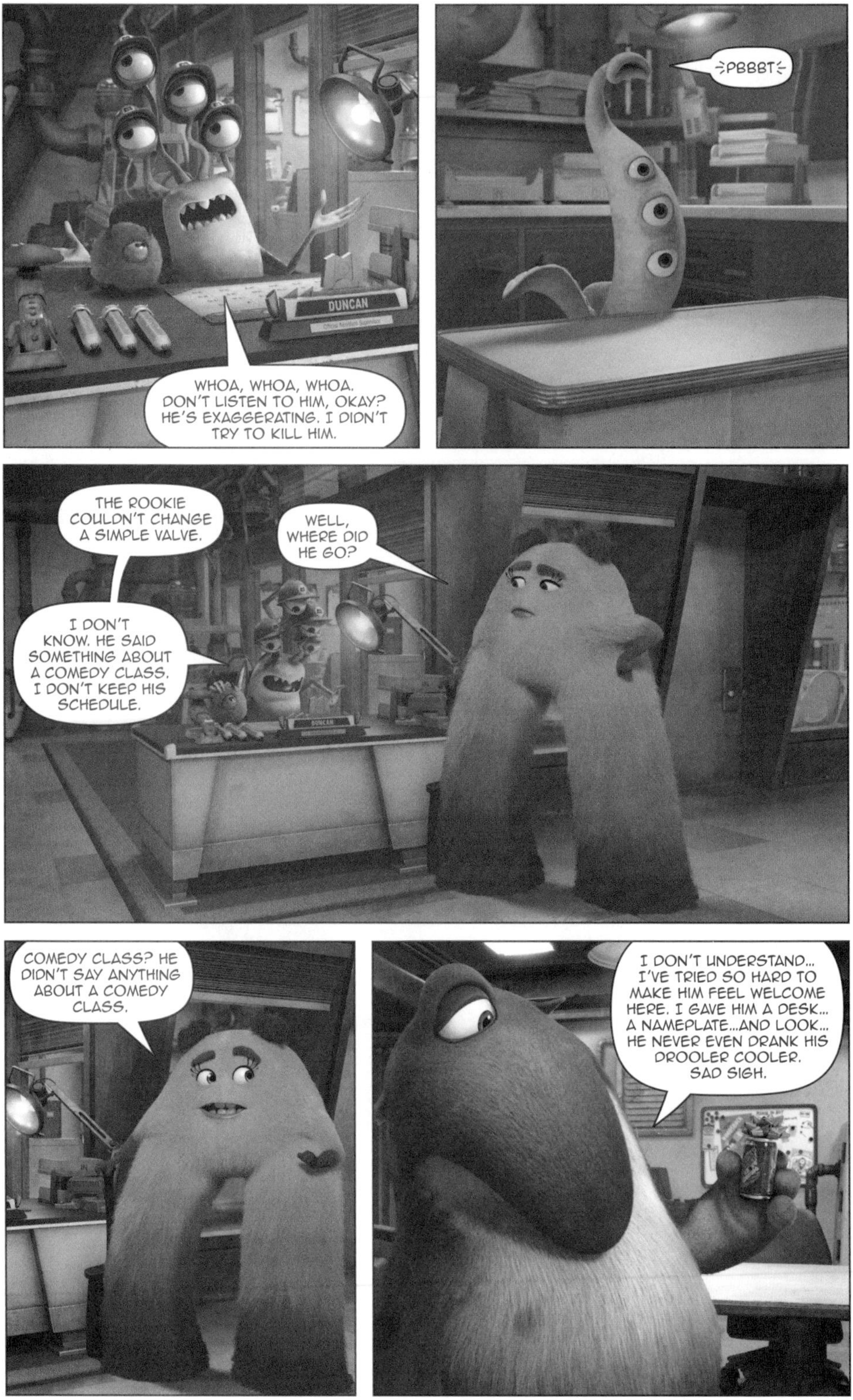
DUNCAN
WHOA, WHOA, WHOA. DON'T LISTEN TO HIM, OKAY? HE'S EXAGGERATING. I DIDN'T TRY TO KILL HIM.
PBBBT
THE ROOKIE COULDN'T CHANGE A SIMPLE VALVE.
WELL, WHERE DID HE GO?
I DON'T KNOW. HE SAID SOMETHING ABOUT A COMEDY CLASS. I DON'T KEEP HIS SCHEDULE.
COMEDY CLASS? HE DIDN'T SAY ANYTHING ABOUT A COMEDY CLASS.
I DON'T UNDERSTAND... I'VE TRIED SO HARD TO MAKE HIM FEEL WELCOME HERE. I GAVE HIM A DESK... A NAMEPLATE...AND LOOK... HE NEVER EVEN DRANK HIS DROOLER COOLER. SAD SIGH.

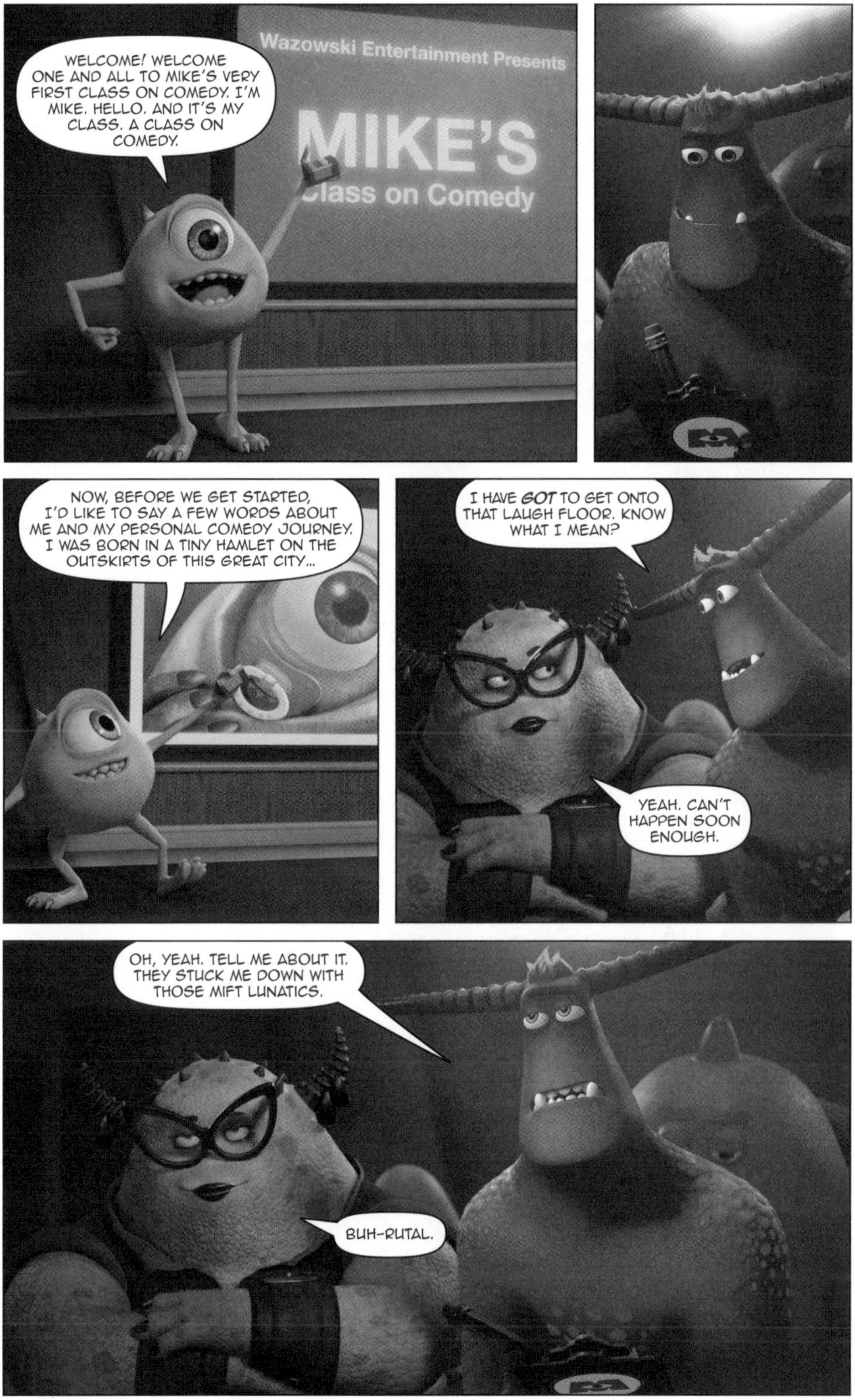
WELCOME! WELCOME ONE AND ALL TO MIKE'S VERY FIRST CLASS ON COMEDY. I'M MIKE. HELLO. AND IT'S MY CLASS. A CLASS ON COMEDY.
Wazowski Entertainment Presents
MIKE'S
Class on Comedy
NOW, BEFORE WE GET STARTED, I'D LIKE TO SAY A FEW WORDS ABOUT ME AND MY PERSONAL COMEDY JOURNEY. I WAS BORN IN A TINY HAMLET ON THE OUTSKIRTS OF THIS GREAT CITY...
I HAVE ***GOT*** TO GET ONTO THAT LAUGH FLOOR. KNOW WHAT I MEAN?
YEAH. CAN'T HAPPEN SOON ENOUGH.
OH, YEAH. TELL ME ABOUT IT. THEY STUCK ME DOWN WITH THOSE MIFT LUNATICS.
BUH-RUTAL.

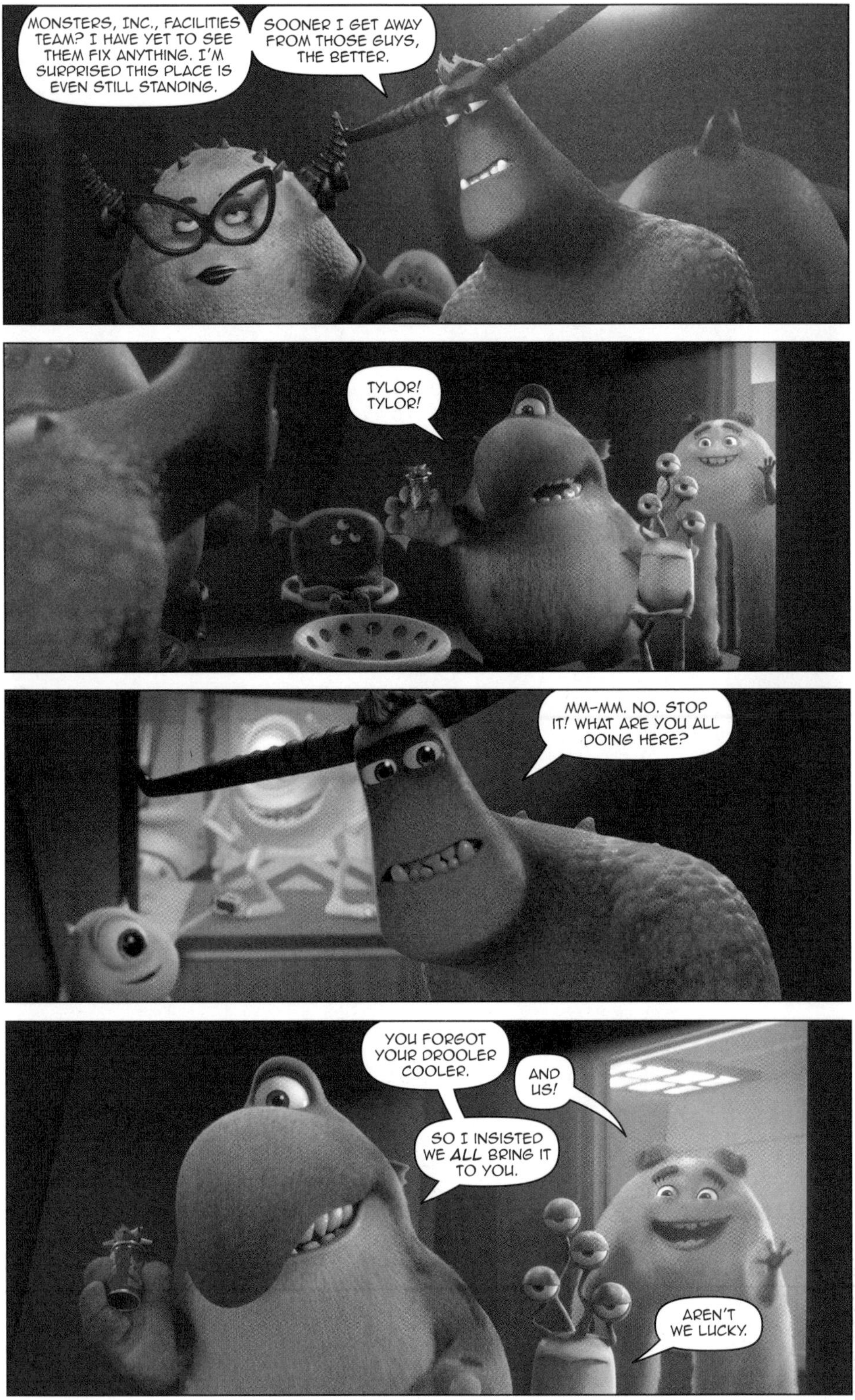
MONSTERS, INC., FACILITIES TEAM? I HAVE YET TO SEE THEM FIX ANYTHING. I'M SURPRISED THIS PLACE IS EVEN STILL STANDING.
SOONER I GET AWAY FROM THOSE GUYS, THE BETTER.
TYLOR! TYLOR!
MM-MM. NO. STOP IT! WHAT ARE YOU ALL DOING HERE?
YOU FORGOT YOUR DROOLER COOLER.
SO I INSISTED WE *ALL* BRING IT TO YOU.
AND US!
AREN'T WE LUCKY.

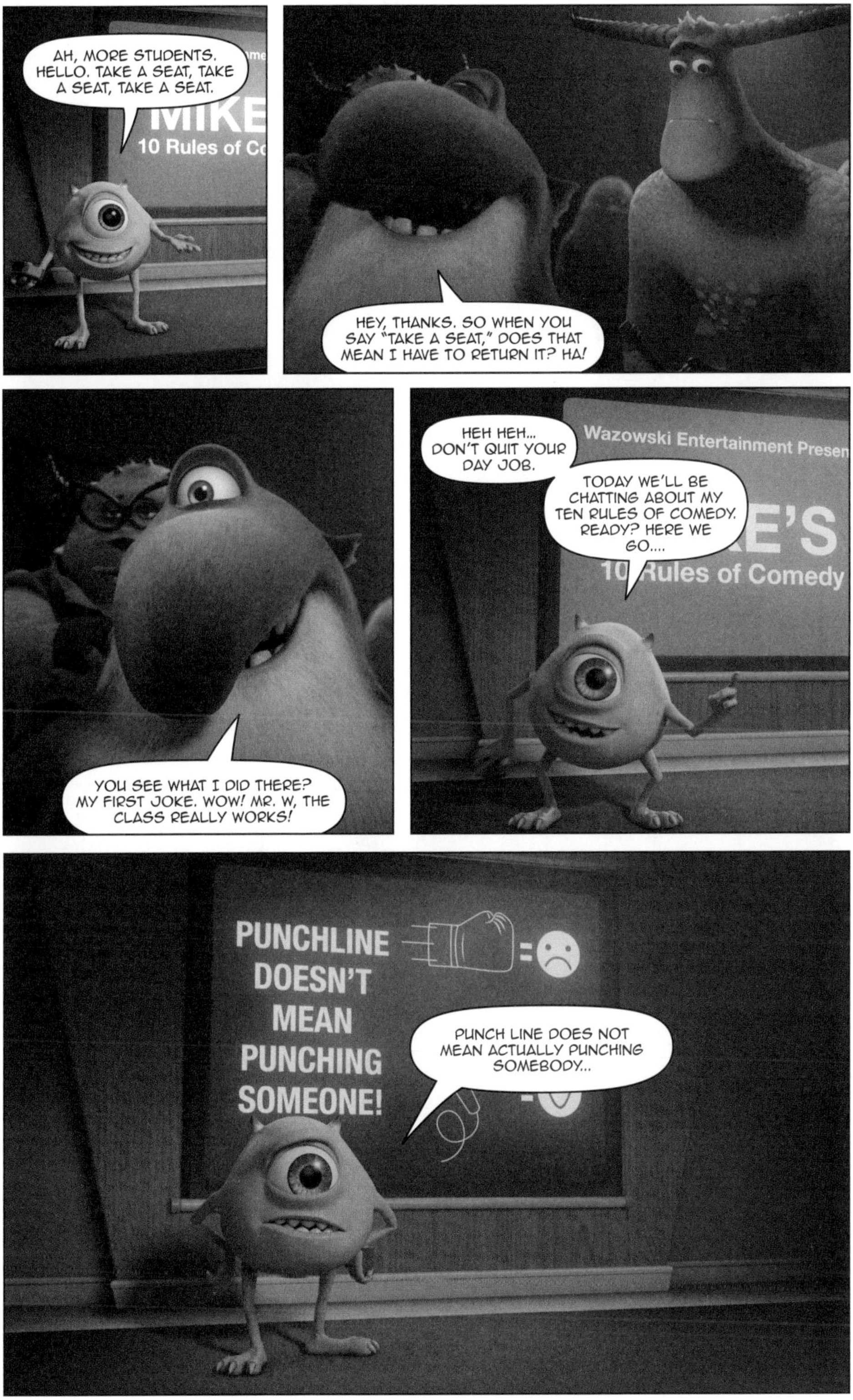
AH, MORE STUDENTS. HELLO. TAKE A SEAT, TAKE A SEAT, TAKE A SEAT.
HEY, THANKS. SO WHEN YOU SAY "TAKE A SEAT," DOES THAT MEAN I HAVE TO RETURN IT? HA!
YOU SEE WHAT I DID THERE? MY FIRST JOKE. WOW! MR. W, THE CLASS REALLY WORKS!
HEH HEH... DON'T QUIT YOUR DAY JOB.
TODAY WE'LL BE CHATTING ABOUT MY TEN RULES OF COMEDY. READY? HERE WE GO....
10 Rules of Comedy
PUNCHLINE DOESN'T MEAN PUNCHING SOMEONE!
PUNCH LINE DOES NOT MEAN ACTUALLY PUNCHING SOMEBODY...

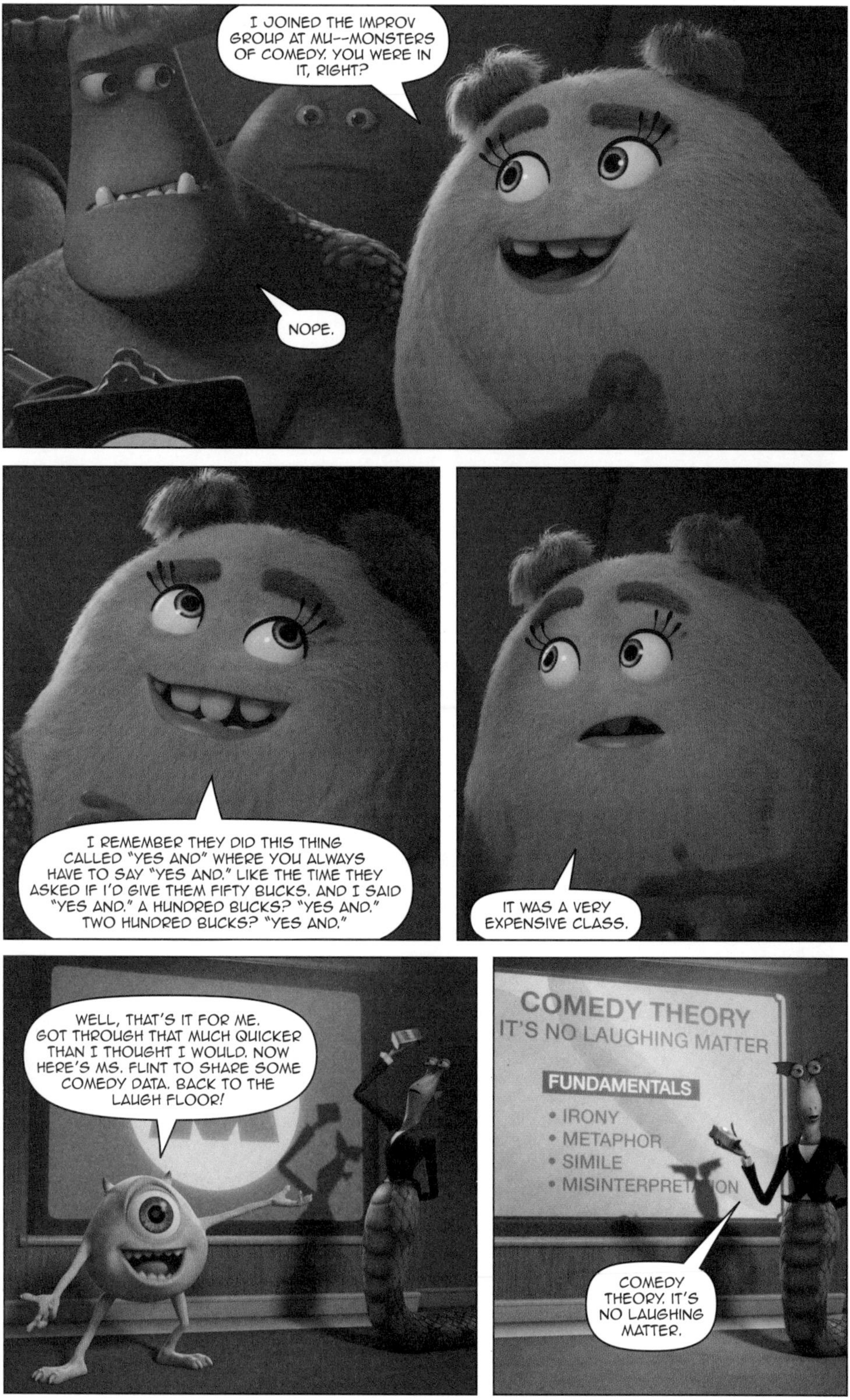
I JOINED THE IMPROV GROUP AT MU--MONSTERS OF COMEDY. YOU WERE IN IT, RIGHT?
NOPE.
I REMEMBER THEY DID THIS THING CALLED "YES AND" WHERE YOU ALWAYS HAVE TO SAY "YES AND." LIKE THE TIME THEY ASKED IF I'D GIVE THEM FIFTY BUCKS. AND I SAID "YES AND." A HUNDRED BUCKS? "YES AND." TWO HUNDRED BUCKS? "YES AND."
IT WAS A VERY EXPENSIVE CLASS.
WELL, THAT'S IT FOR ME. GOT THROUGH THAT MUCH QUICKER THAN I THOUGHT I WOULD. NOW HERE'S MS. FLINT TO SHARE SOME COMEDY DATA. BACK TO THE LAUGH FLOOR!
COMEDY THEORY
IT'S NO LAUGHING MATTER
FUNDAMENTALS
• IRONY
• METAPHOR
• SIMILE
• MISINTERPRET
COMEDY THEORY. IT'S NO LAUGHING MATTER.

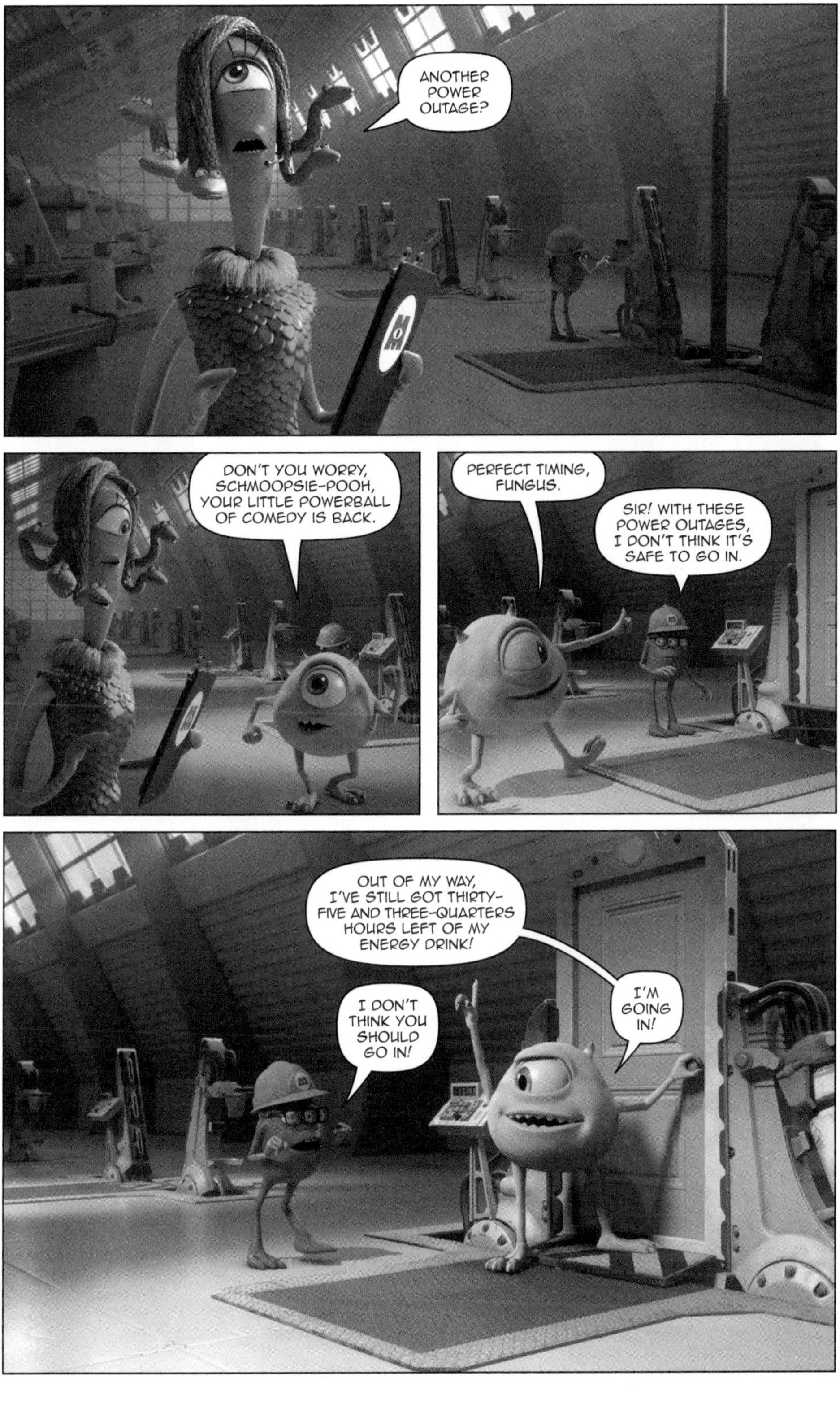

ANOTHER POWER OUTAGE?
DON'T YOU WORRY, SCHMOOPSIE-POOH, YOUR LITTLE POWERBALL OF COMEDY IS BACK.
PERFECT TIMING, FUNGUS.
SIR! WITH THESE POWER OUTAGES, I DON'T THINK IT'S SAFE TO GO IN.
OUT OF MY WAY, I'VE STILL GOT THIRTY-FIVE AND THREE-QUARTERS HOURS LEFT OF MY ENERGY DRINK!
I DON'T THINK YOU SHOULD GO IN!
I'M GOING IN!

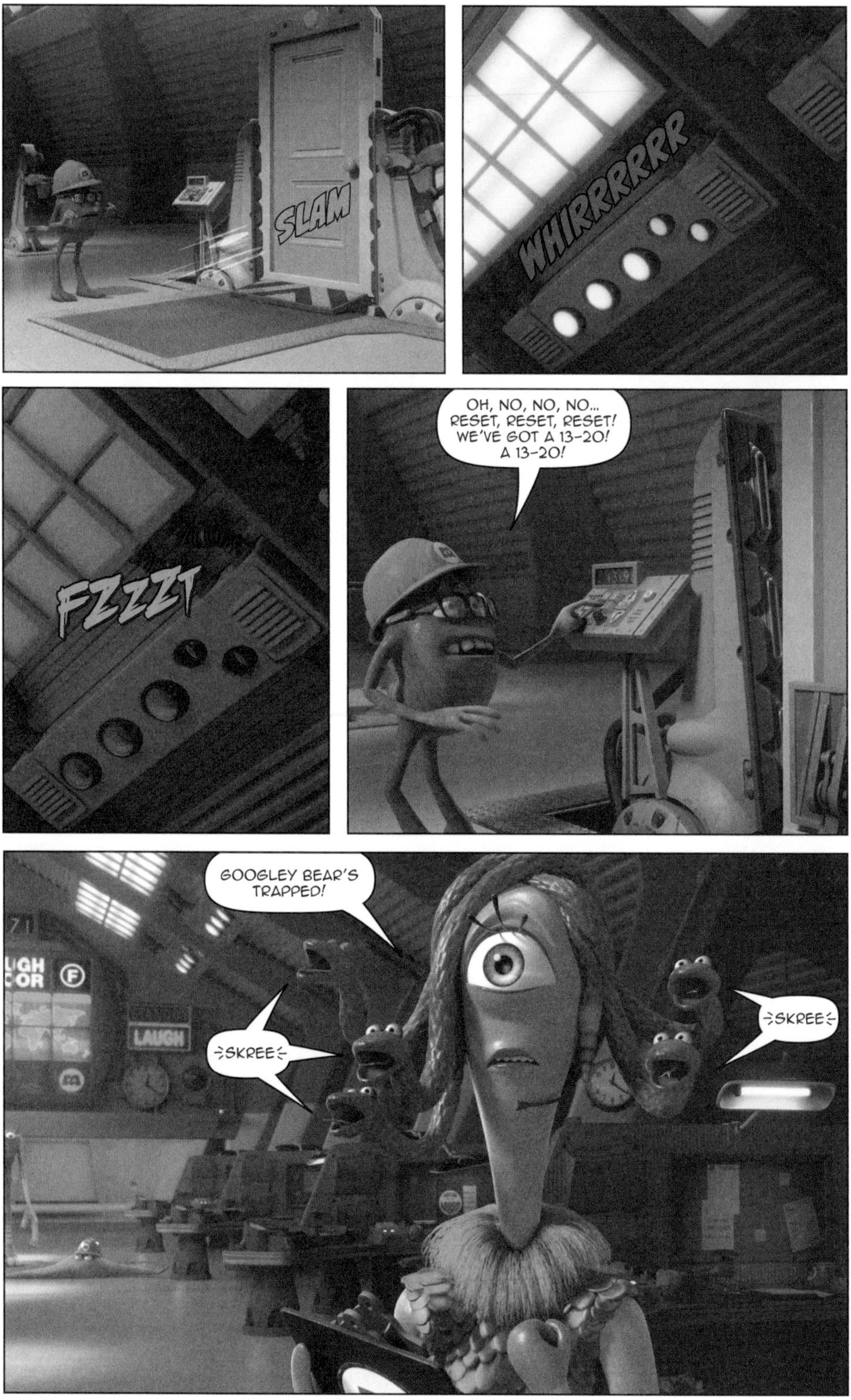
SLAM
WHIRRRRRR
FZZZT
OH, NO, NO, NO... RESET, RESET, RESET! WE'VE GOT A 13-20! A 13-20!
GOOGLEY BEAR'S TRAPPED!
SKREE
SKREE

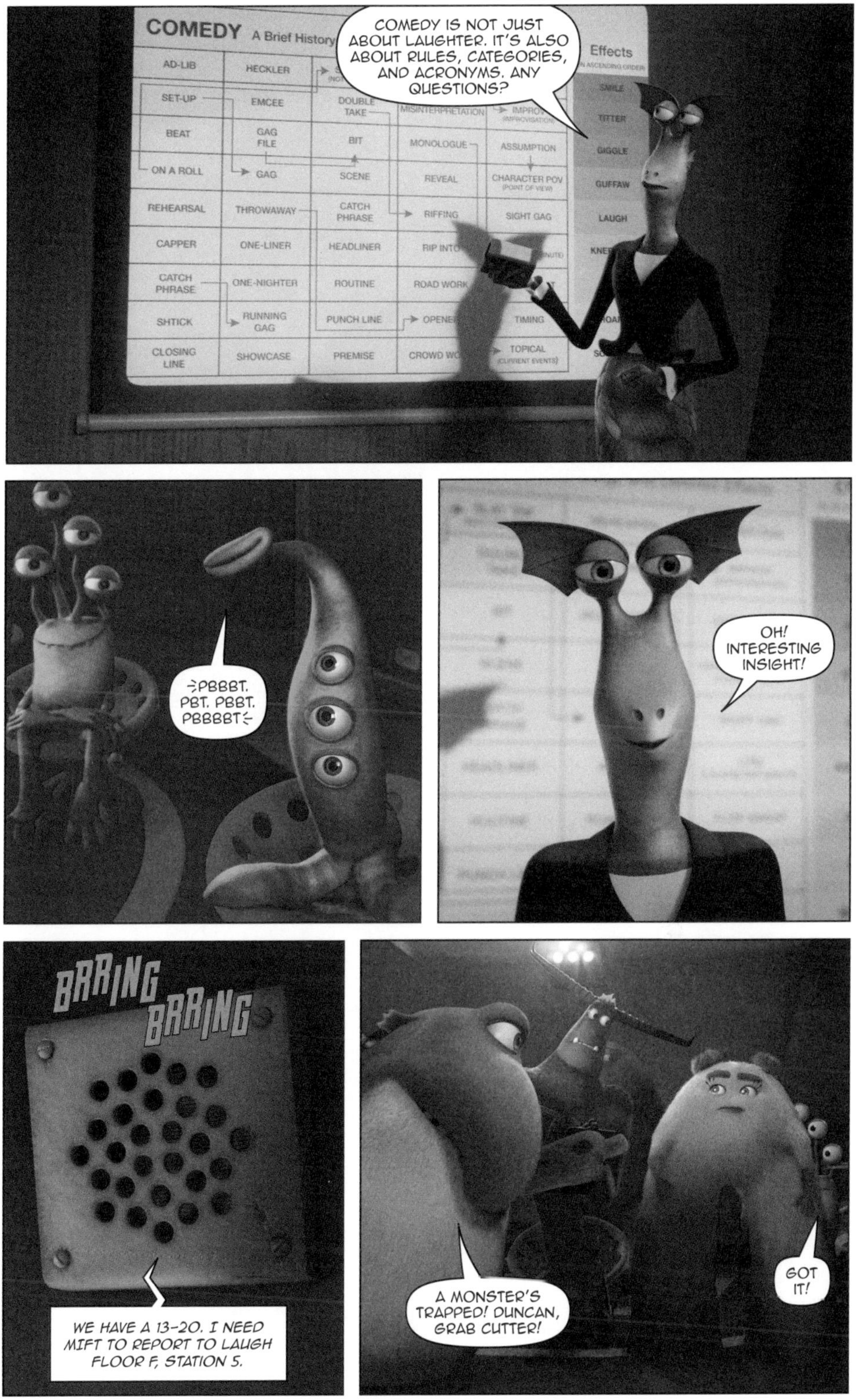

COMEDY A Brief History
COMEDY IS NOT JUST ABOUT LAUGHTER. IT'S ALSO ABOUT RULES, CATEGORIES, AND ACRONYMS. ANY QUESTIONS?
=PBBBT. PBT. PBBT. PBBBBT=
OH! INTERESTING INSIGHT!
BRRING BRRING
WE HAVE A 13-20. I NEED MIFT TO REPORT TO LAUGH FLOOR F, STATION 5.
A MONSTER'S TRAPPED! DUNCAN, GRAB CUTTER!
GOT IT!

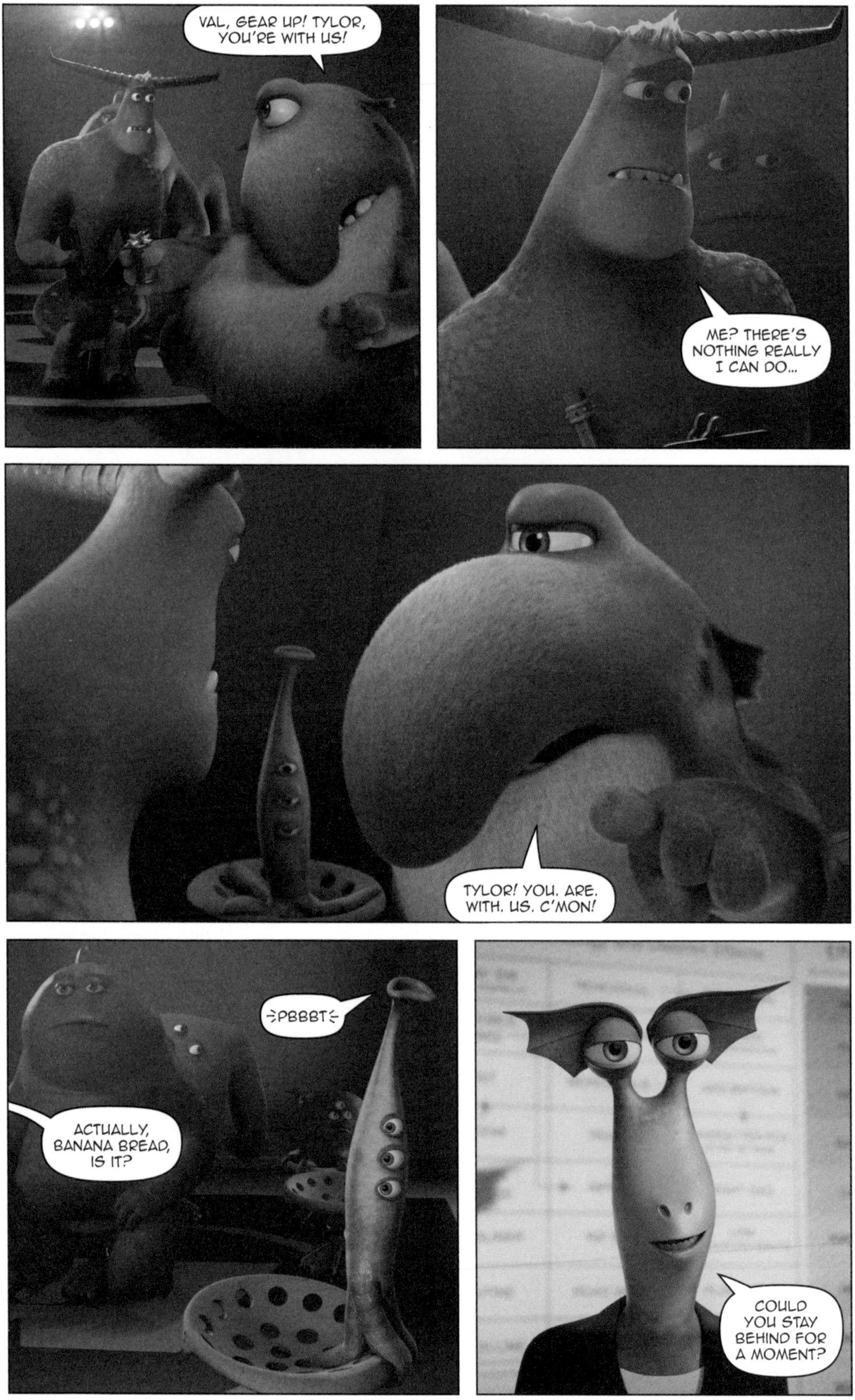
VAL, GEAR UP! TYLOR, YOU'RE WITH US!
ME? THERE'S NOTHING REALLY I CAN DO...
TYLOR! YOU. ARE. WITH. US. C'MON!
ACTUALLY, BANANA BREAD, IS IT?
PBBBT
COULD YOU STAY BEHIND FOR A MOMENT?

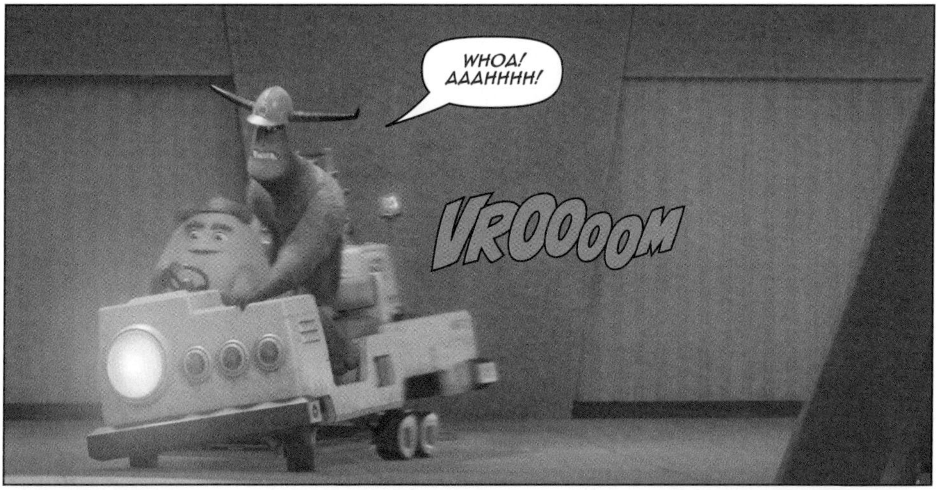
WHOA!
AAAHHHH!
VROOOOOM

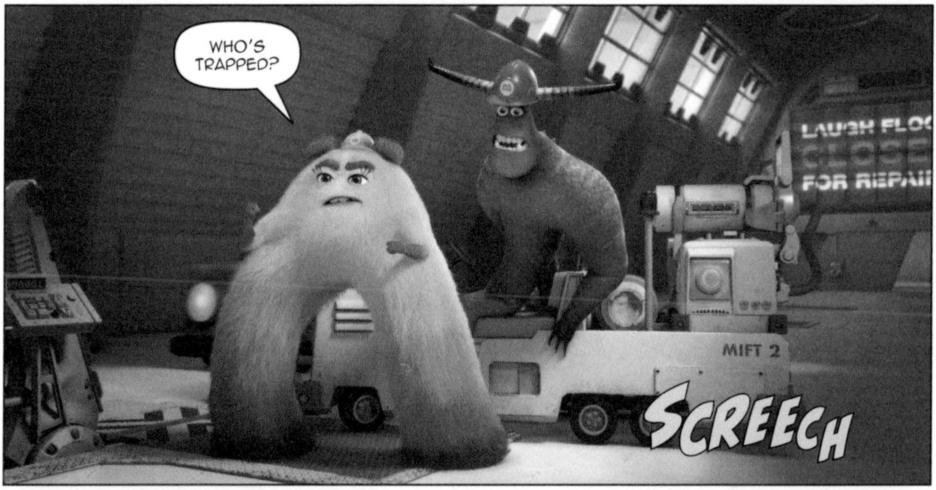
WHO'S TRAPPED?
MIFT 2
SCREECH

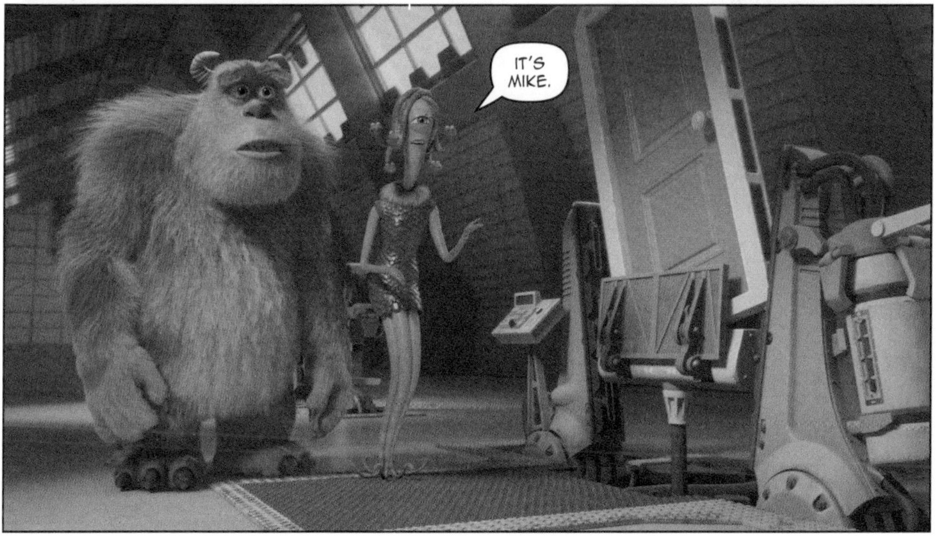
IT'S MIKE.

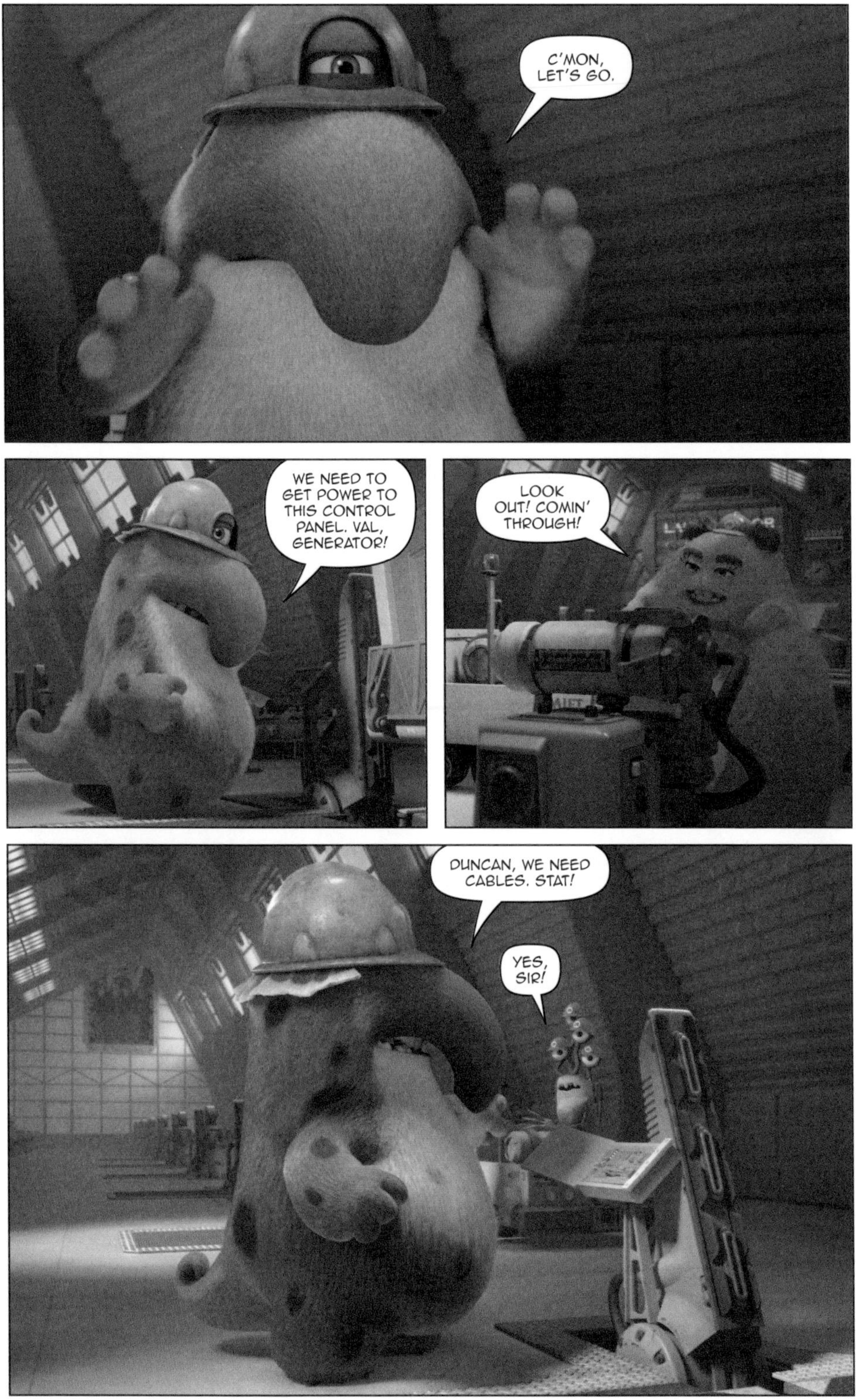
C'MON, LET'S GO.
WE NEED TO GET POWER TO THIS CONTROL PANEL. VAL, GENERATOR!
LOOK OUT! COMIN' THROUGH!
DUNCAN, WE NEED CABLES. STAT!
YES, SIR!

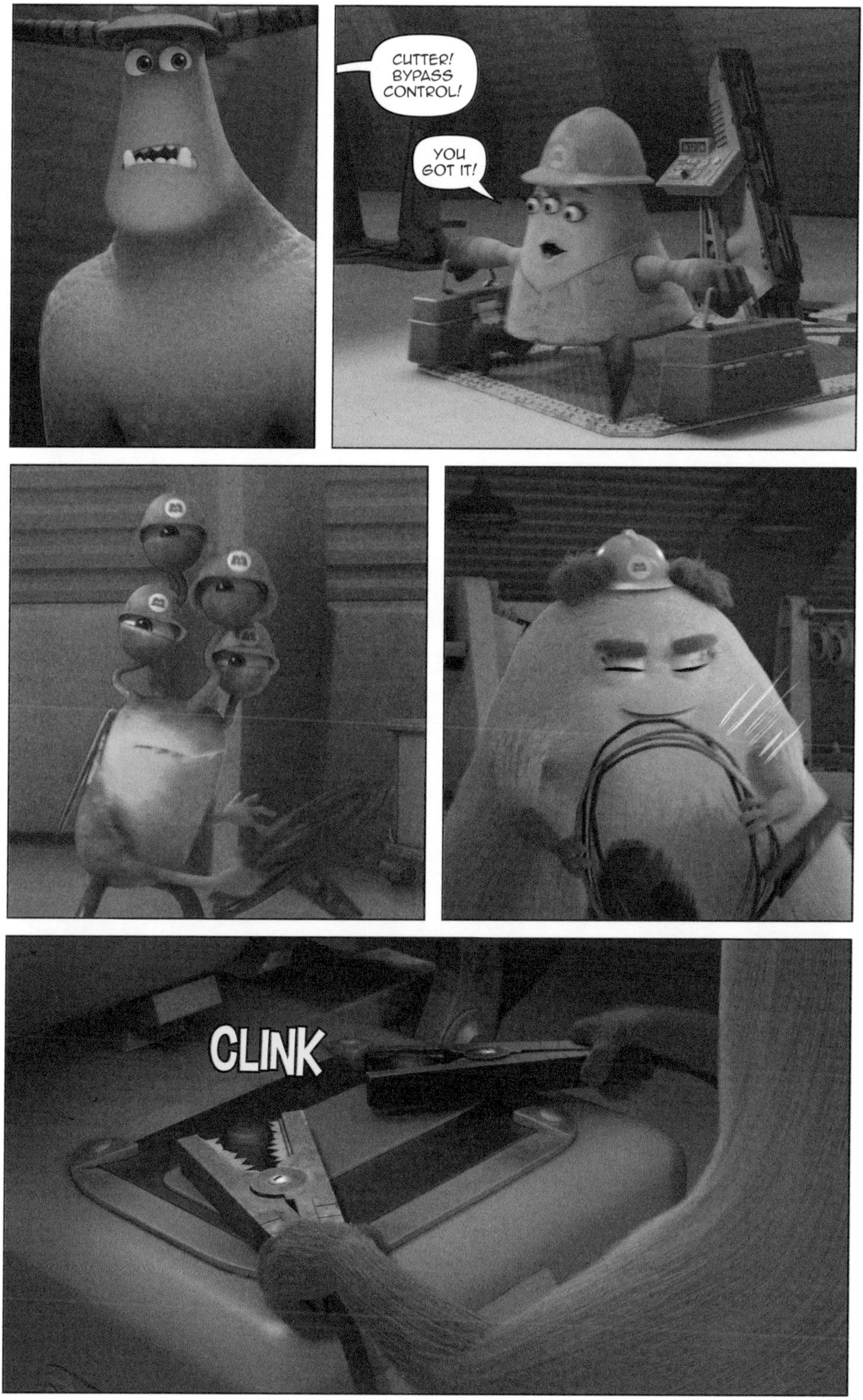
CUTTER! BYPASS CONTROL!
YOU GOT IT!
CLINK

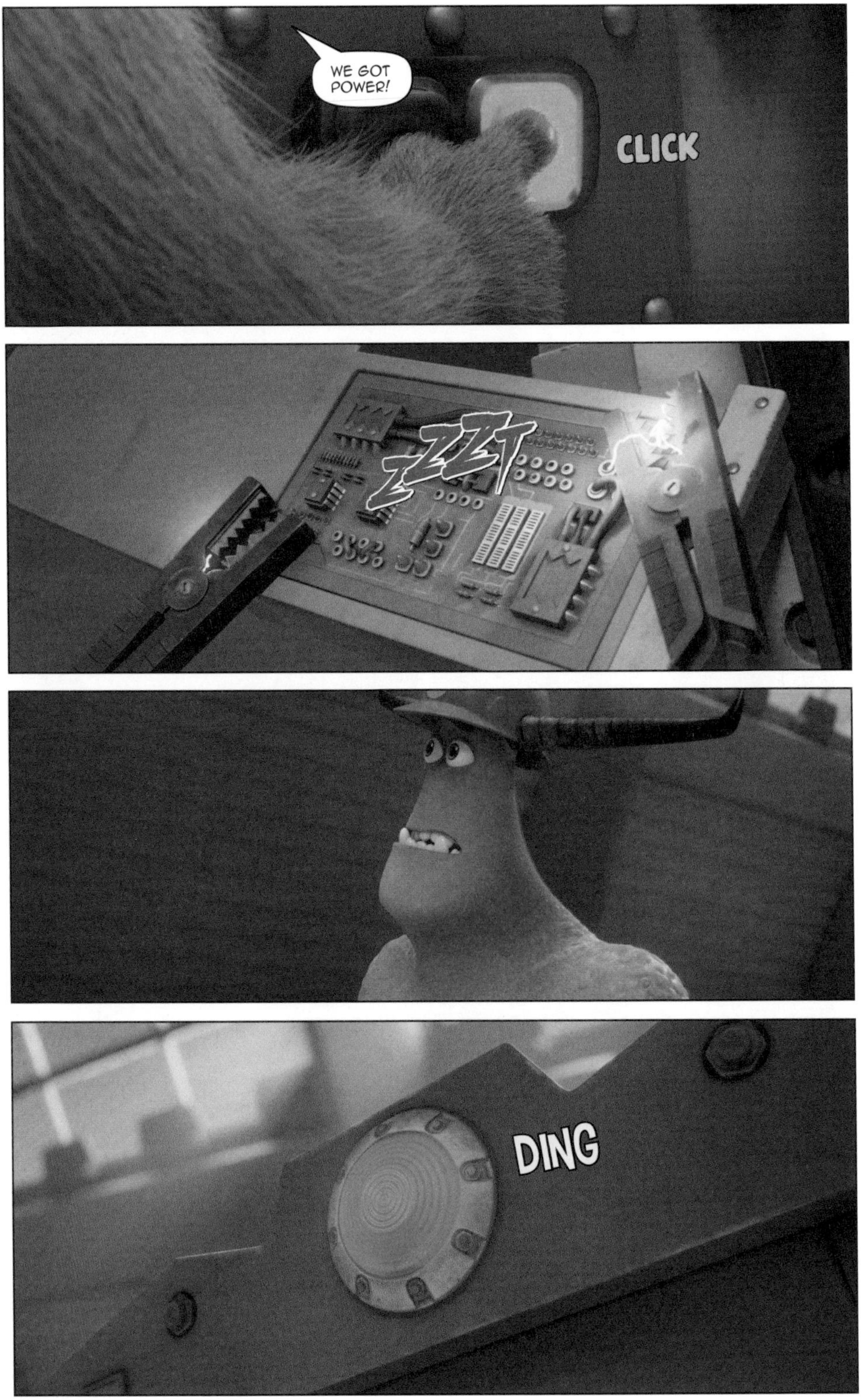
WE GOT POWER!
CLICK
ZZZT
DING

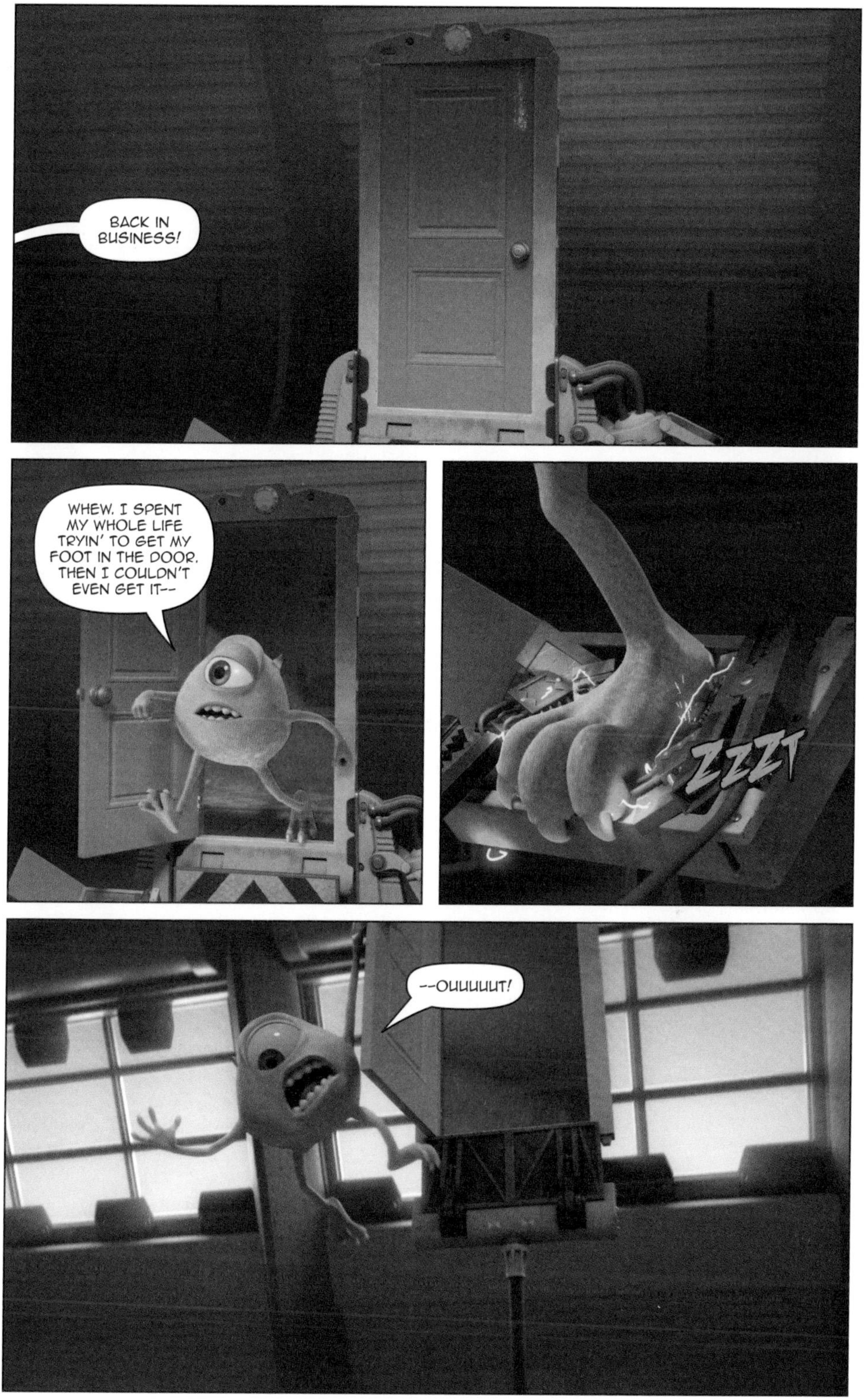
BACK IN BUSINESS!
WHEW. I SPENT MY WHOLE LIFE TRYIN' TO GET MY FOOT IN THE DOOR. THEN I COULDN'T EVEN GET IT--
ZZZT
--OUUUUUT!

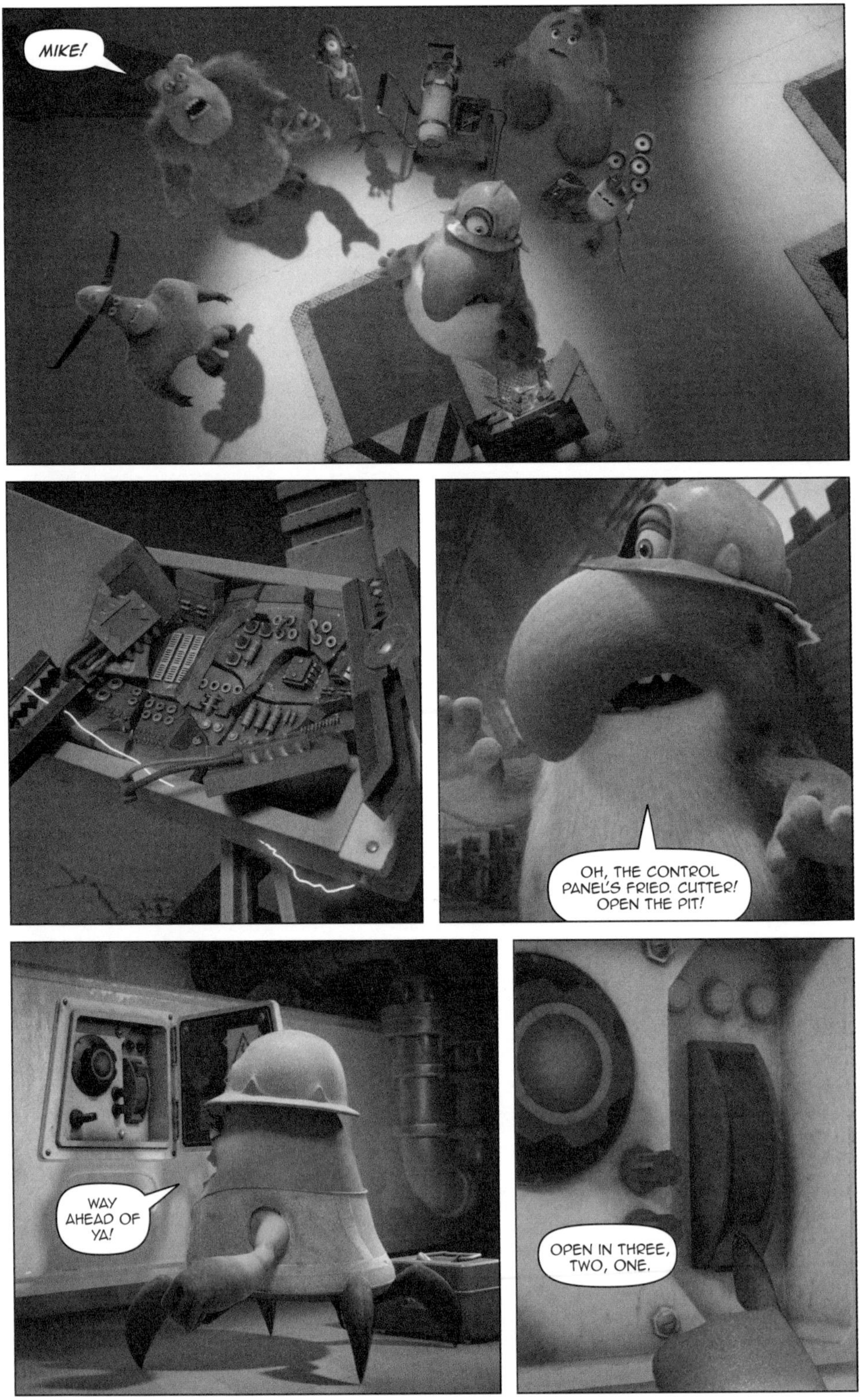
MIKE!
OH, THE CONTROL PANEL'S FRIED. CUTTER! OPEN THE PIT!
WAY AHEAD OF YA!
OPEN IN THREE, TWO, ONE.

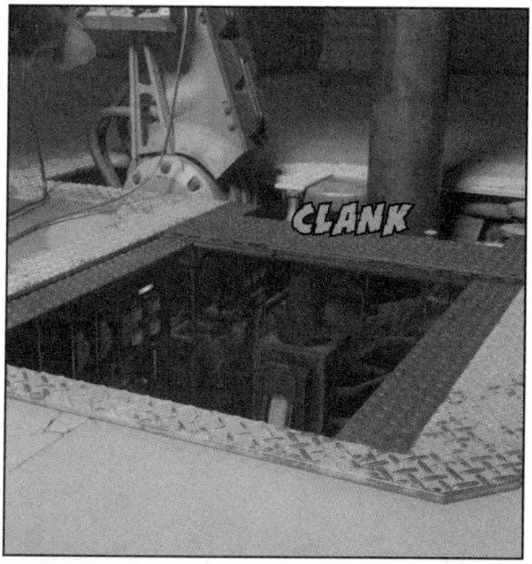
CLANK

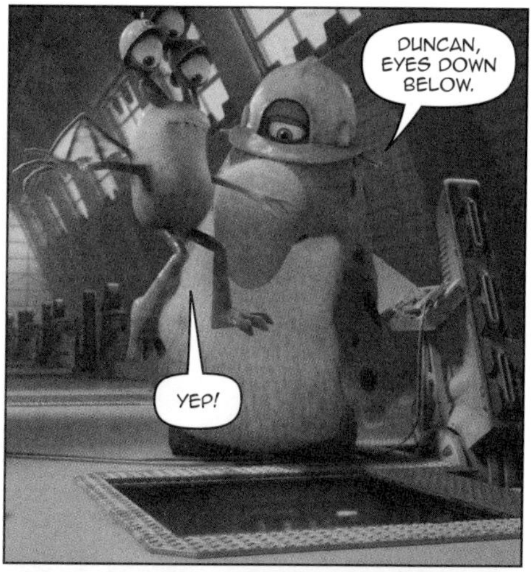
DUNCAN, EYES DOWN BELOW.
YEP!

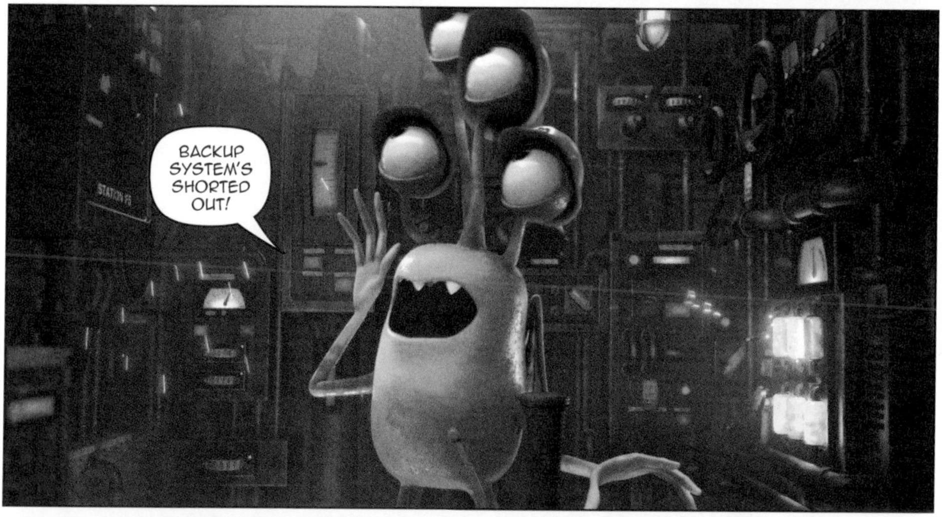
BACKUP SYSTEM'S SHORTED OUT!

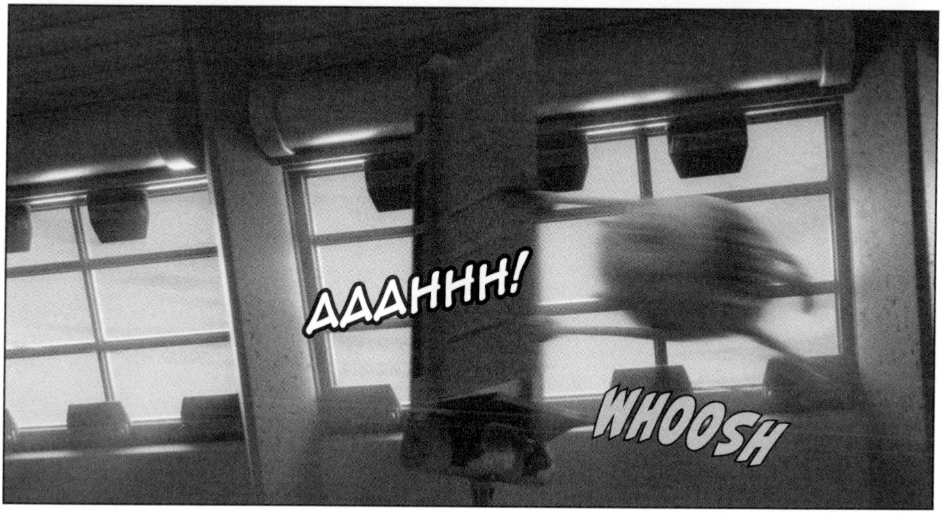
AAAHHH!
WHOOSH

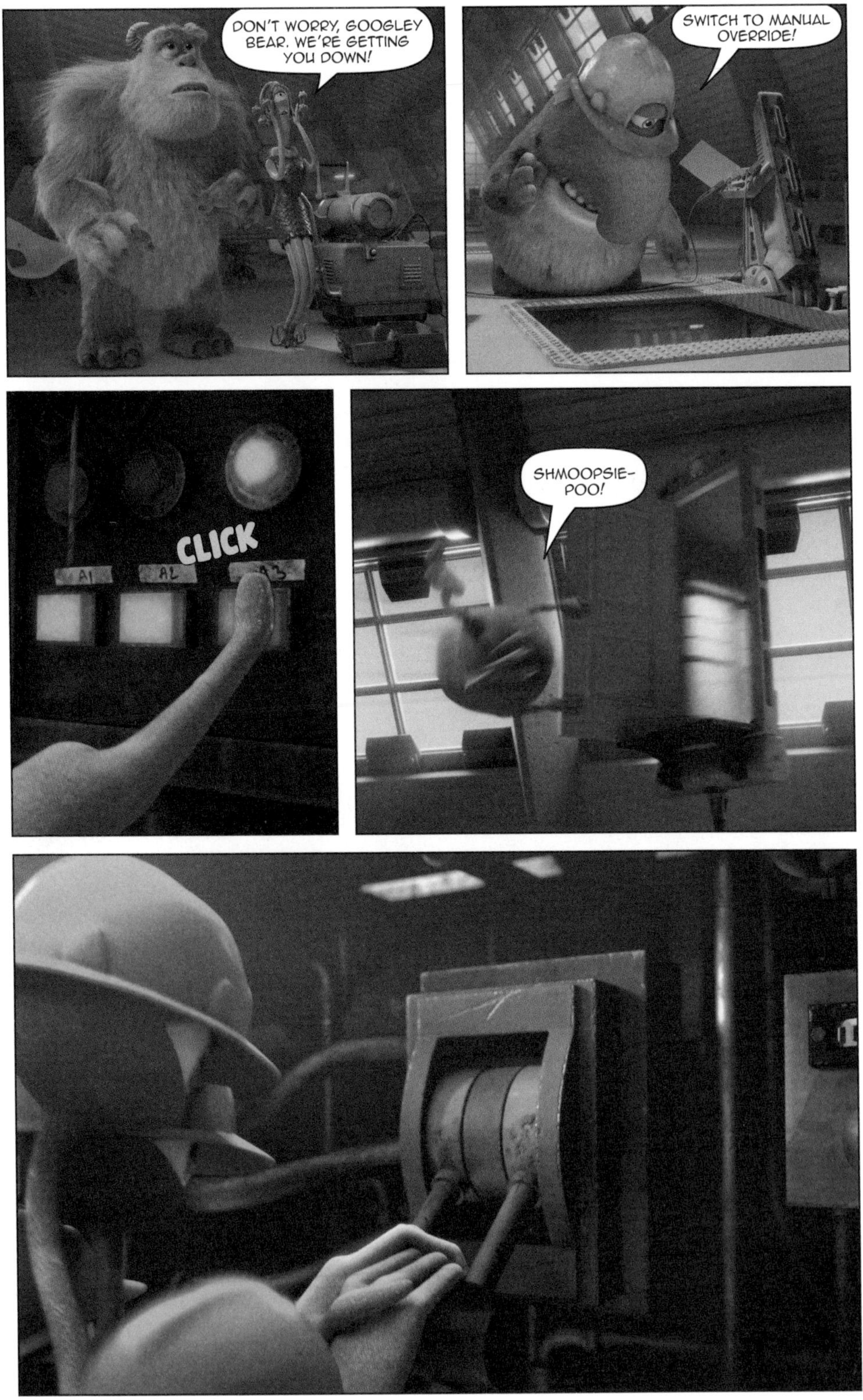
DON'T WORRY, GOOGLEY BEAR. WE'RE GETTING YOU DOWN!
SWITCH TO MANUAL OVERRIDE!
CLICK
SHMOOPSIE-POO!

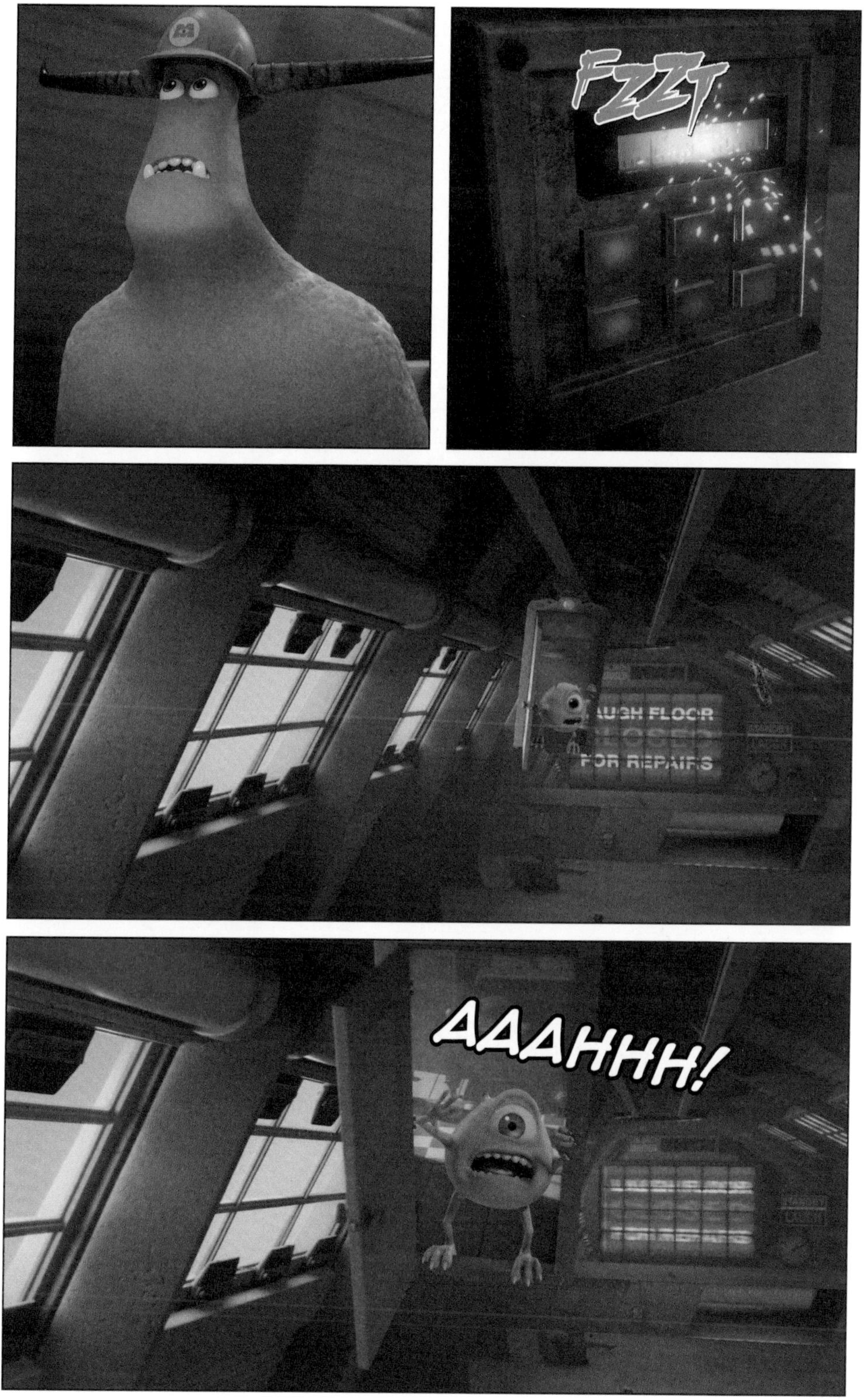
FZZT
AUGH FLOOR
FOR REPAIRS
AAAHHH!

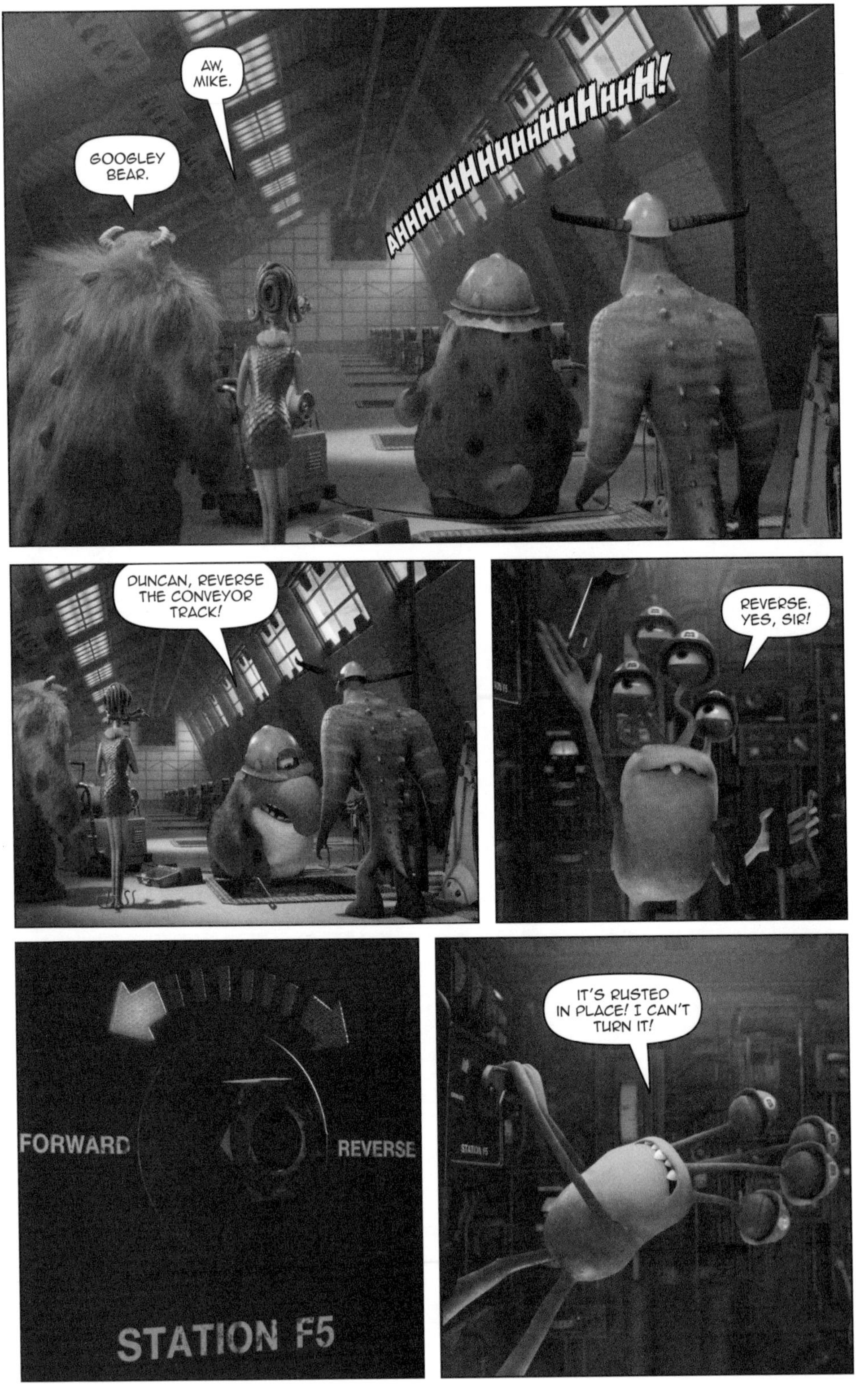
GOOGLEY BEAR.
AW, MIKE.
AHHHHHHHHHHHHHHHHHHHH!
DUNCAN, REVERSE THE CONVEYOR TRACK!
REVERSE. YES, SIR!
FORWARD
REVERSE
STATION F5
STATION F5
IT'S RUSTED IN PLACE! I CAN'T TURN IT!

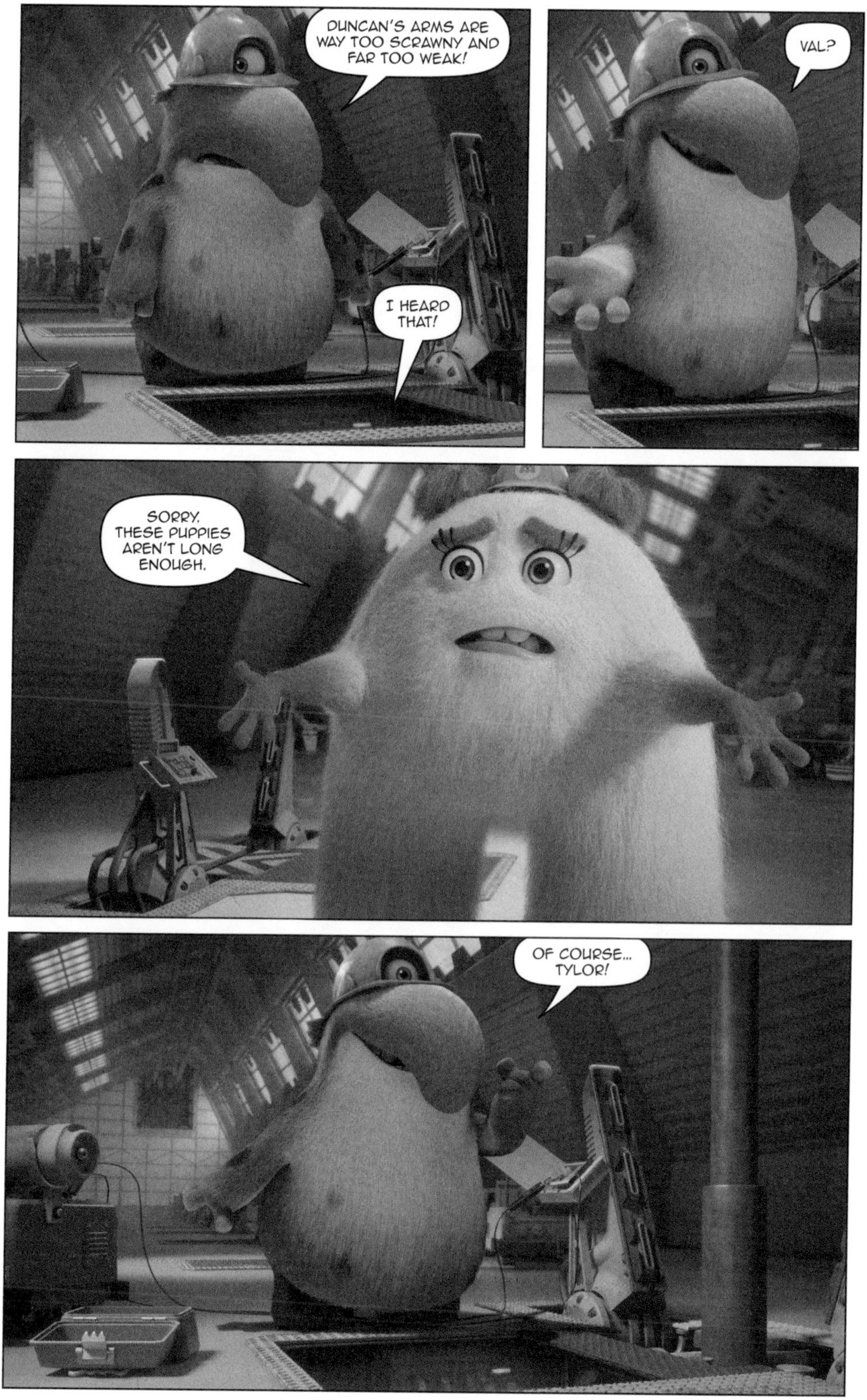
DUNCAN'S ARMS ARE WAY TOO SCRAWNY AND FAR TOO WEAK!
I HEARD THAT!
VAL?
SORRY. THESE PUPPIES AREN'T LONG ENOUGH.
OF COURSE... TYLOR!

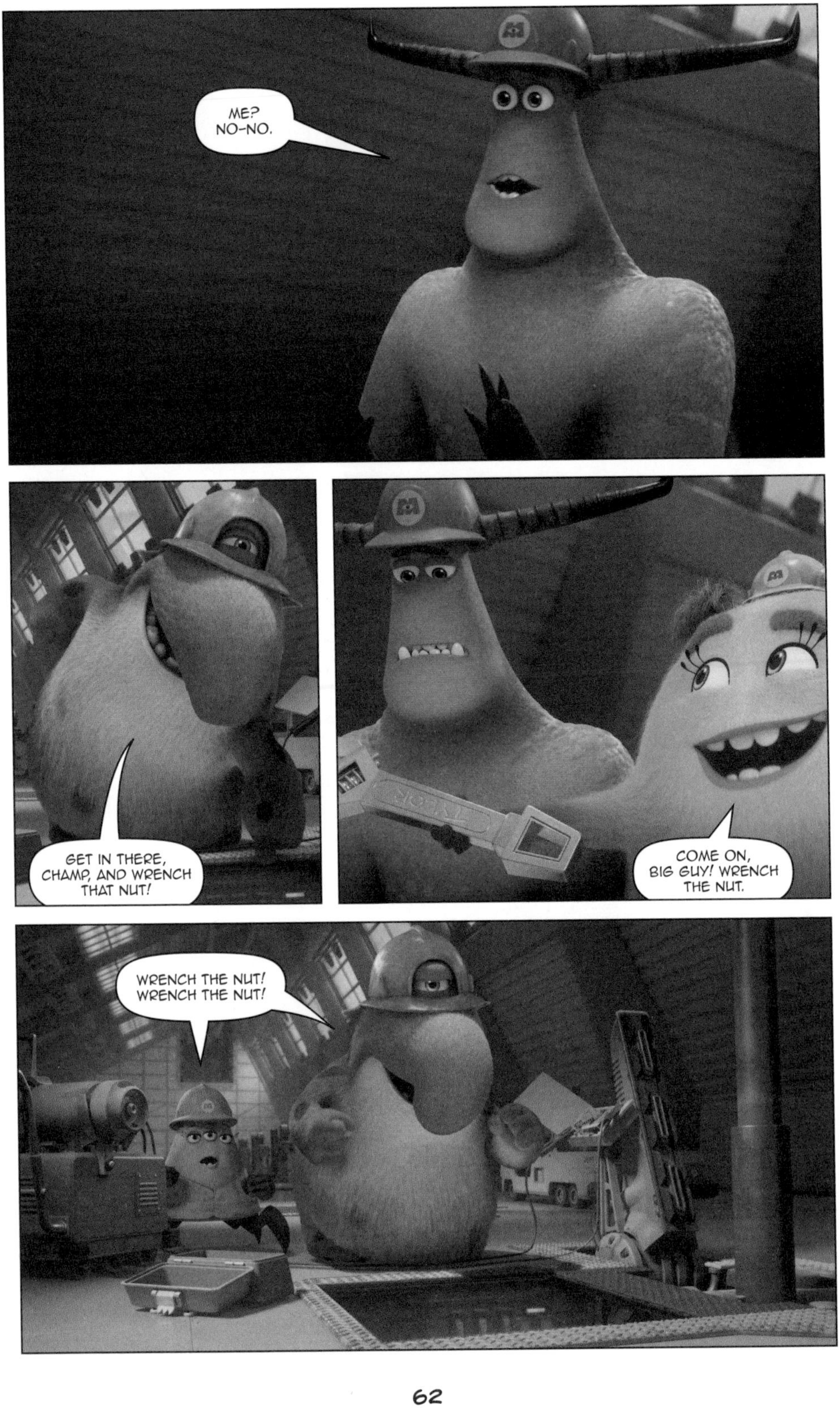
ME? NO-NO.
GET IN THERE, CHAMP, AND WRENCH THAT NUT!
COME ON, BIG GUY! WRENCH THE NUT.
WRENCH THE NUT! WRENCH THE NUT!

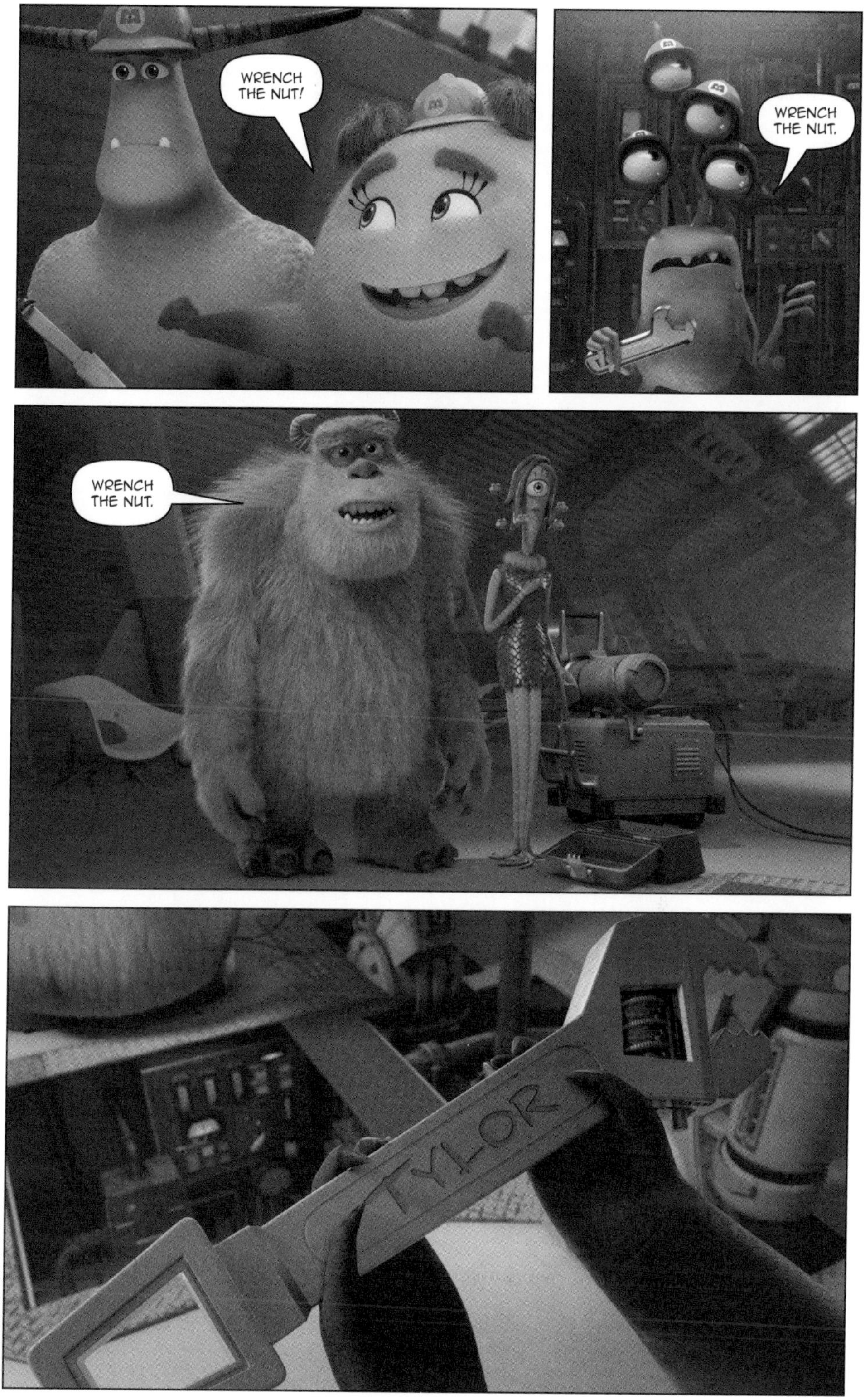
WRENCH THE NUT!
WRENCH THE NUT.
WRENCH THE NUT.
TYLOR

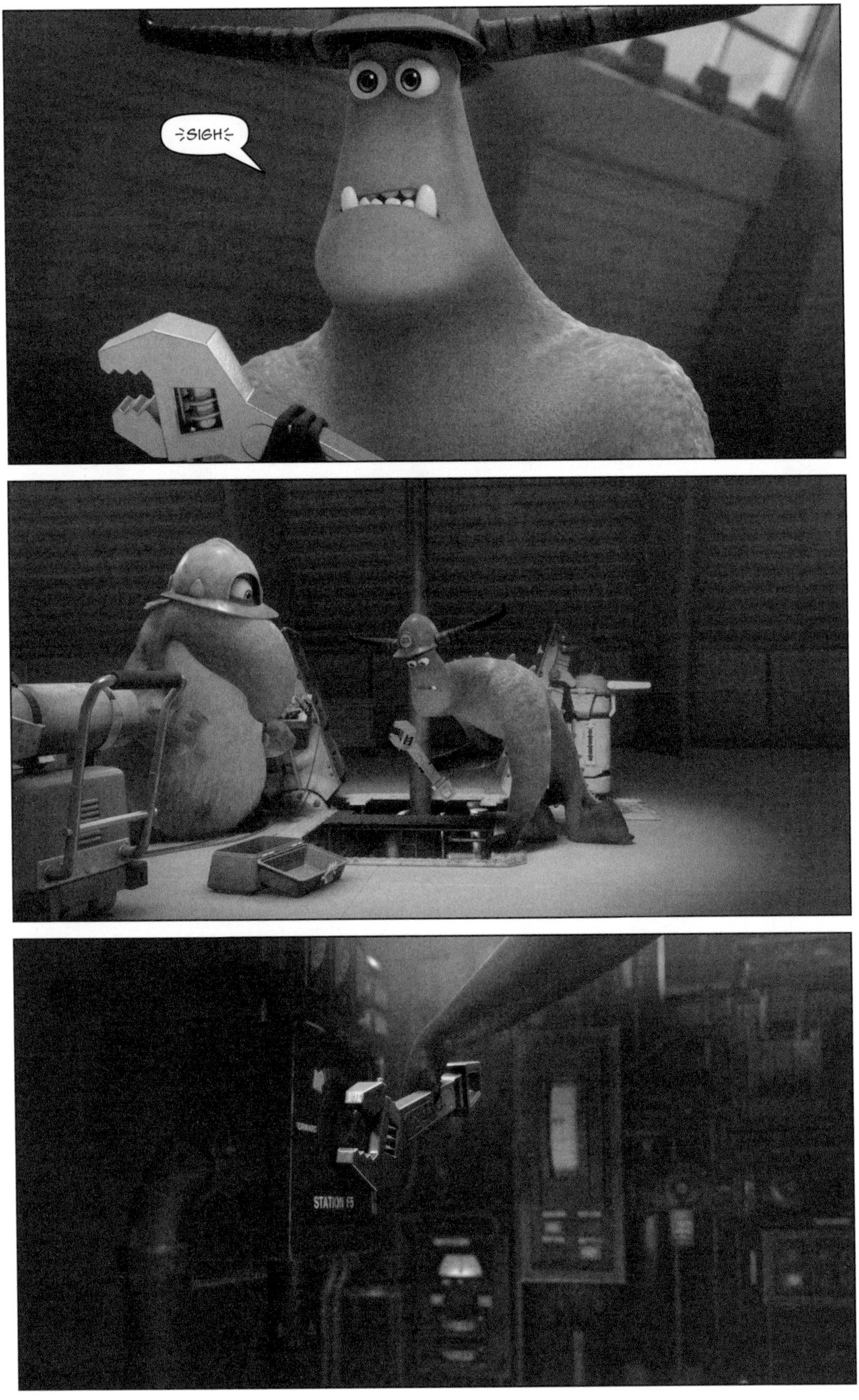
SIGH
STATION F5

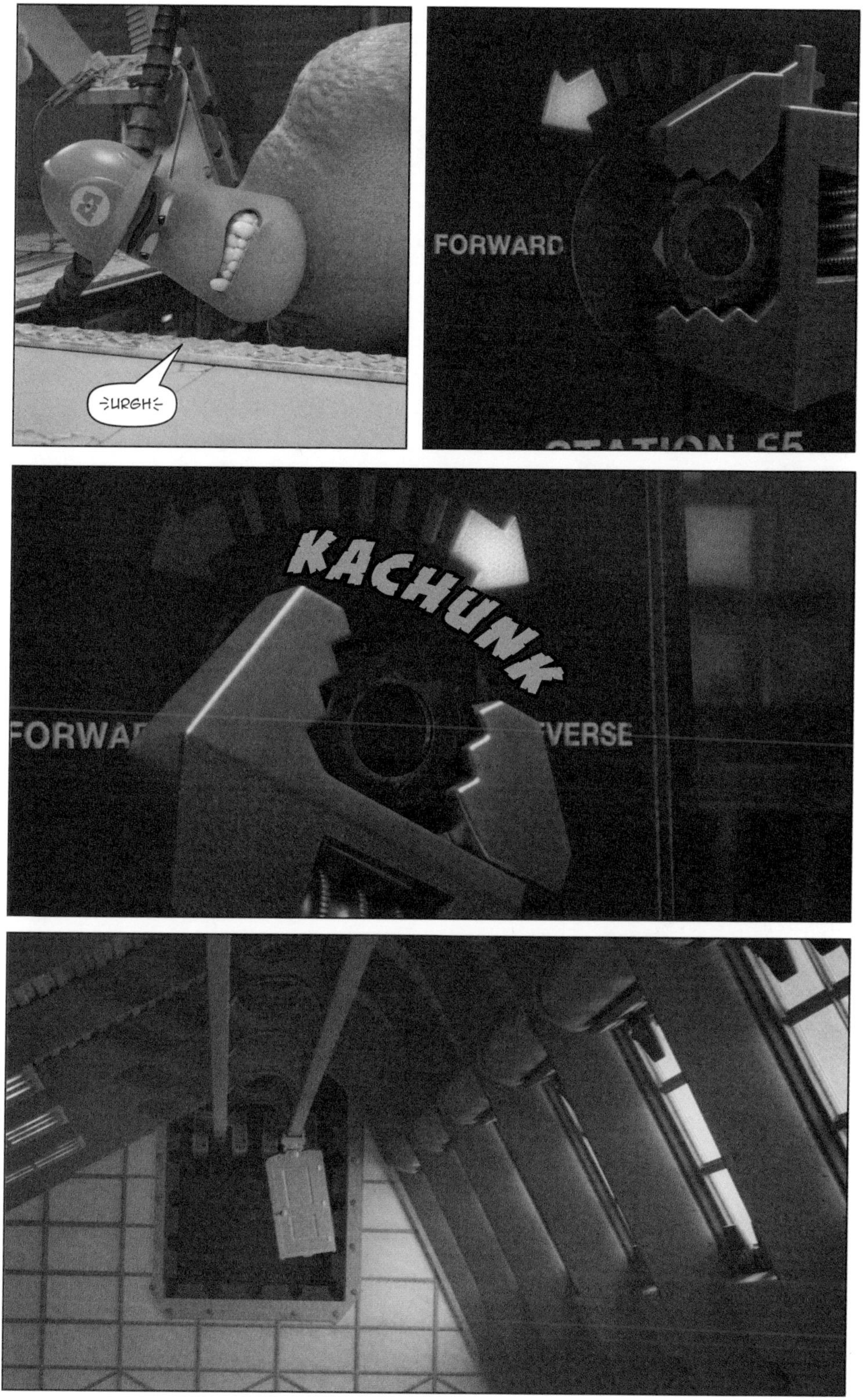
URGH
FORWARD
KACHUNK

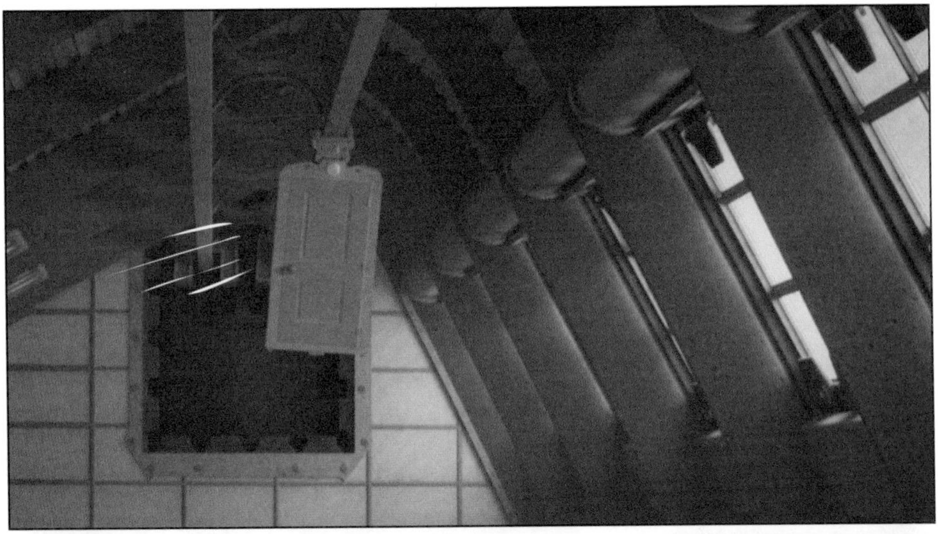

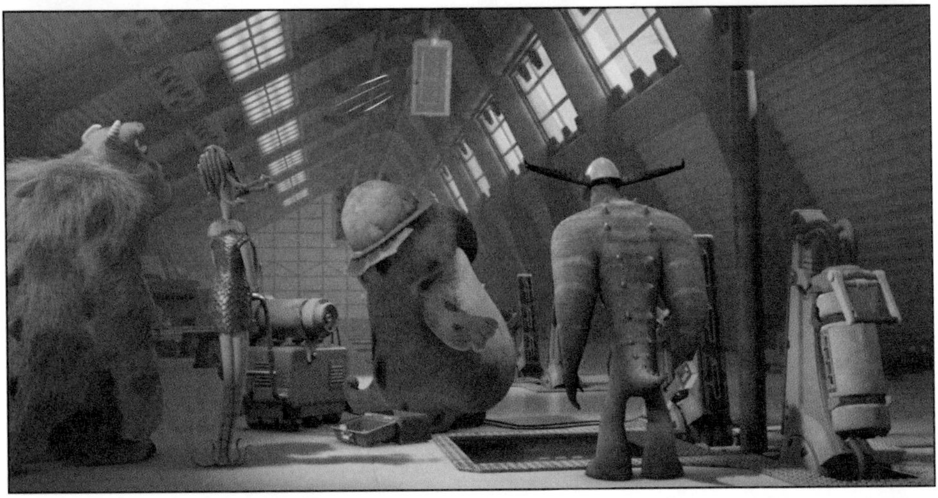

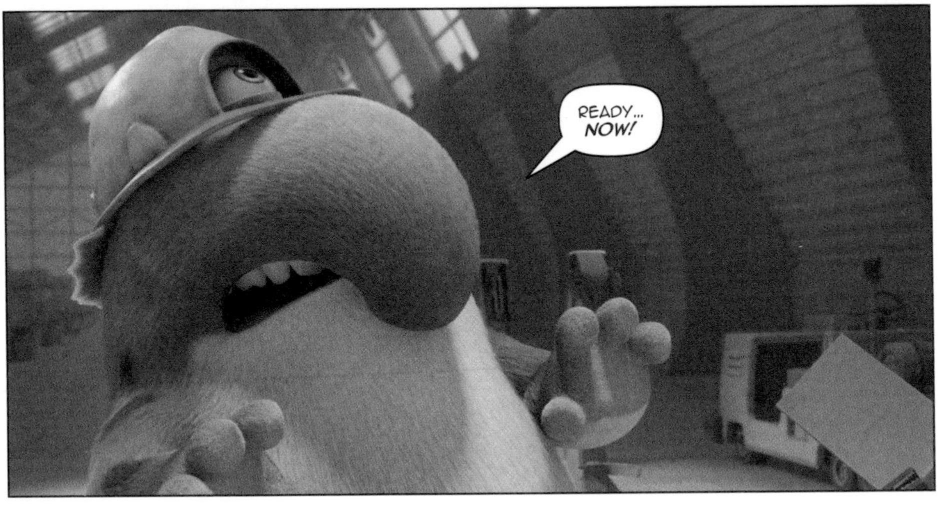
READY... NOW!

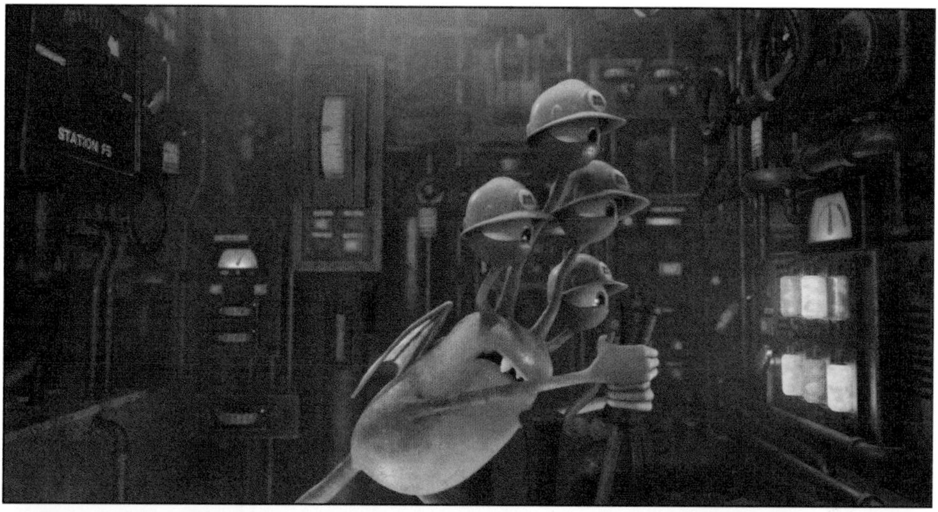
STATION F5

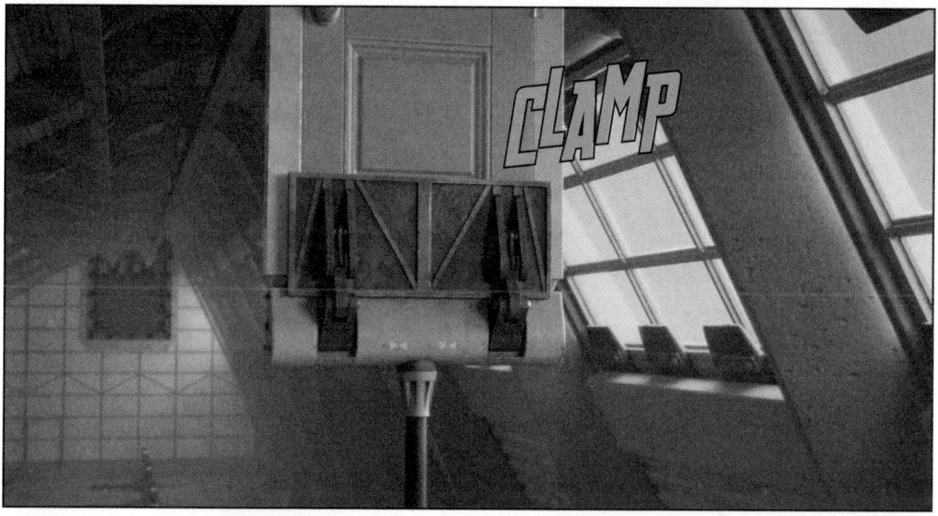
CLAMP

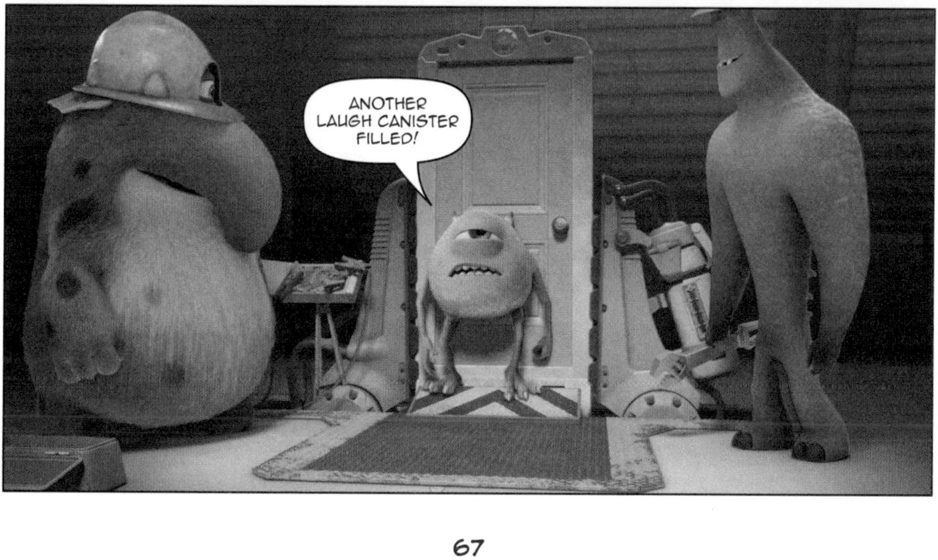
ANOTHER LAUGH CANISTER FILLED!

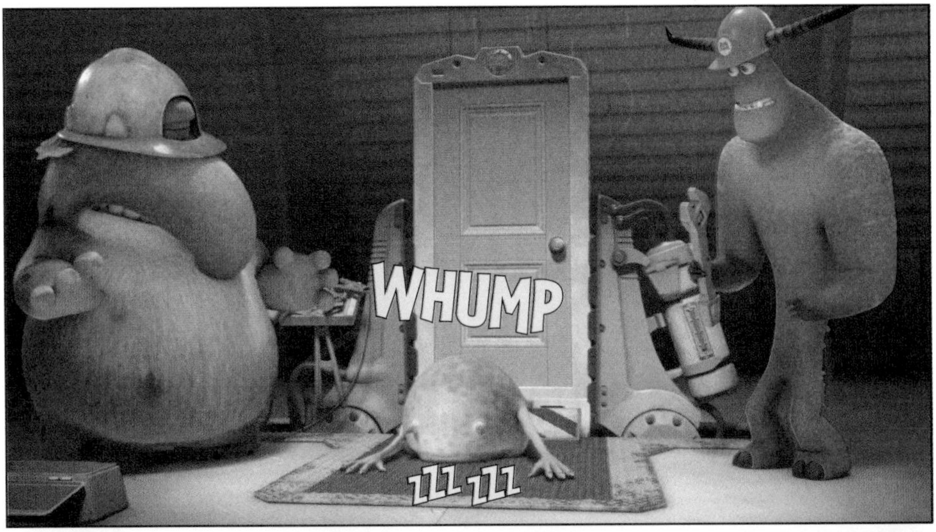
WHUMP
ZZZ ZZZ

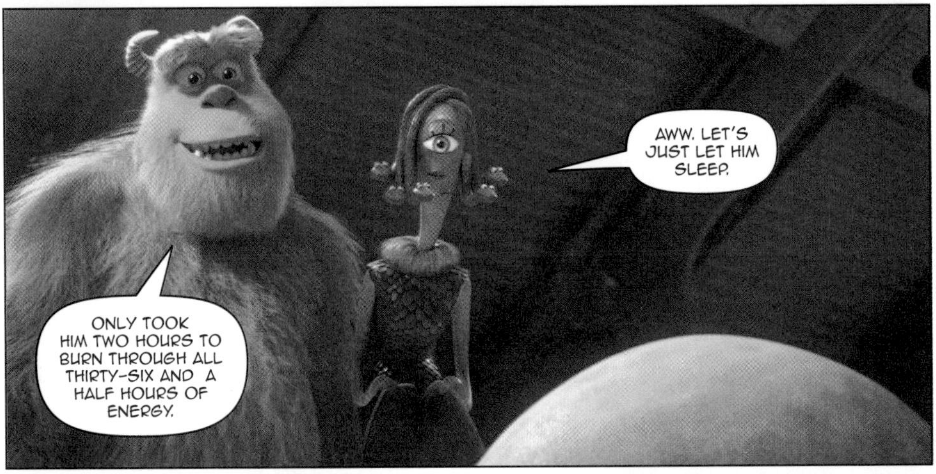
AWW. LET'S JUST LET HIM SLEEP.
ONLY TOOK HIM TWO HOURS TO BURN THROUGH ALL THIRTY-SIX AND A HALF HOURS OF ENERGY.

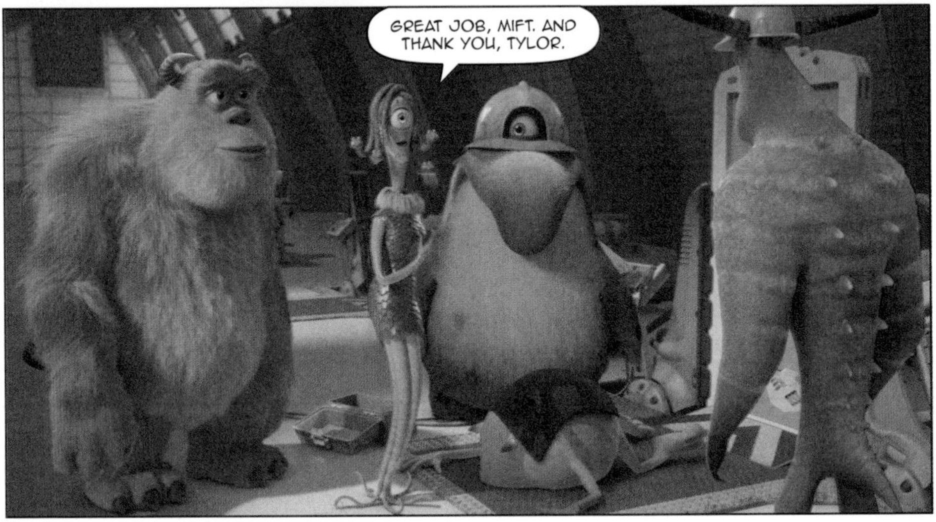
GREAT JOB, MIFT. AND THANK YOU, TYLOR.

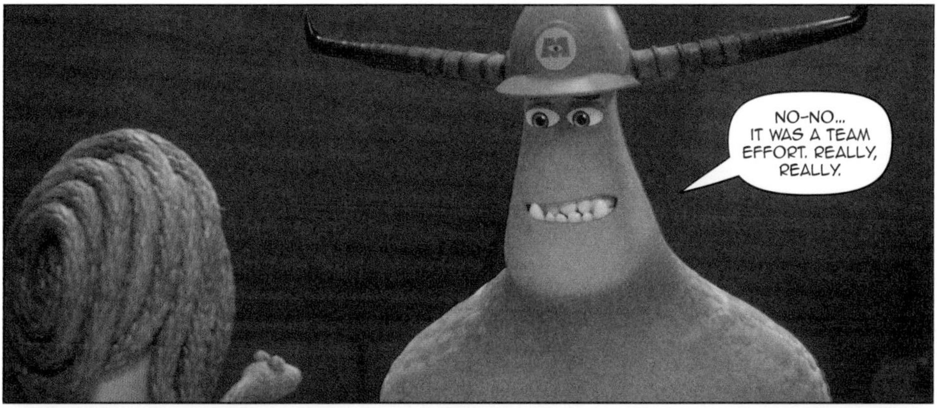
NO-NO... IT WAS A TEAM EFFORT. REALLY, REALLY.

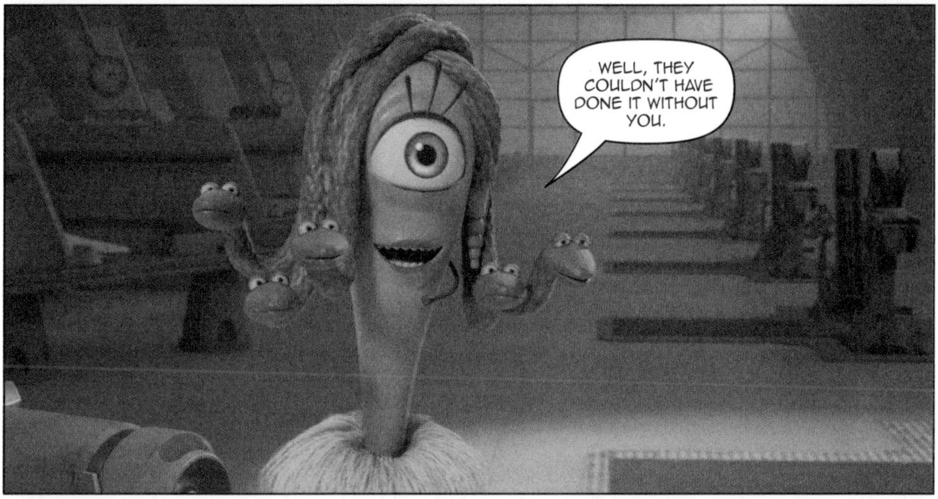
WELL, THEY COULDN'T HAVE DONE IT WITHOUT YOU.

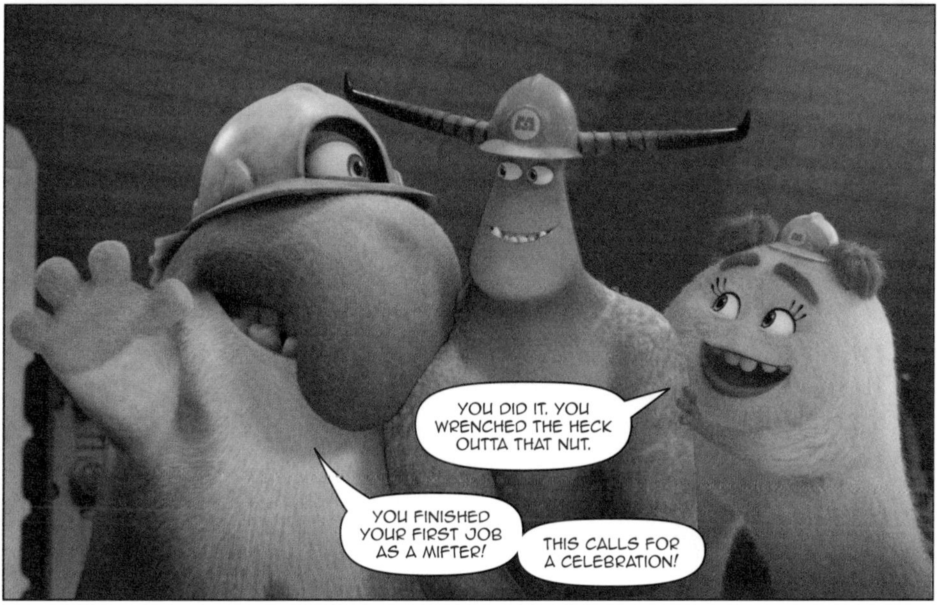
YOU DID IT. YOU WRENCHED THE HECK OUTTA THAT NUT.
YOU FINISHED YOUR FIRST JOB AS A MIFTER!
THIS CALLS FOR A CELEBRATION!

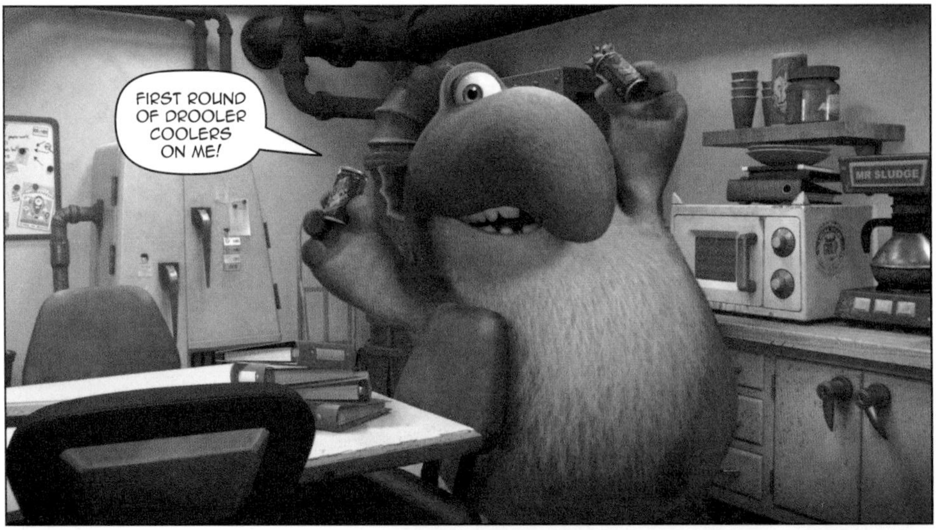
FIRST ROUND OF DROOLER COOLERS ON ME!
MR SLUDGE

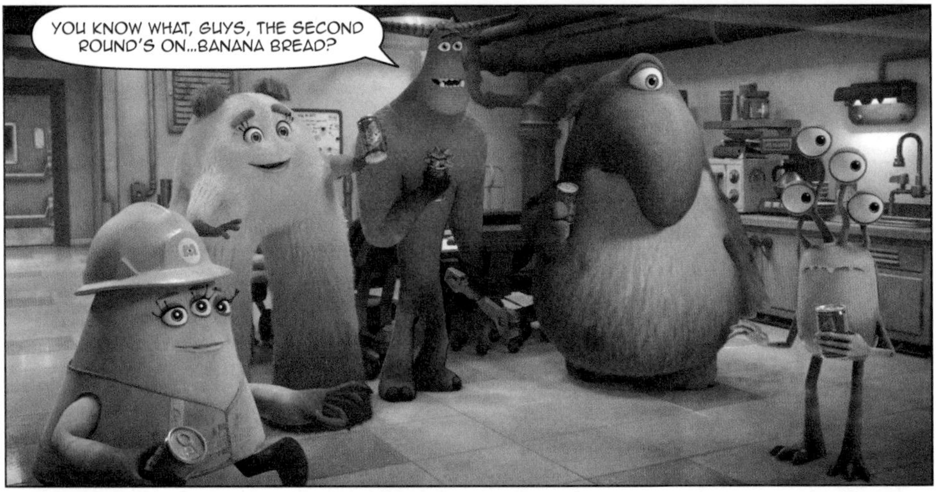
YOU KNOW WHAT, GUYS, THE SECOND ROUND'S ON...BANANA BREAD?

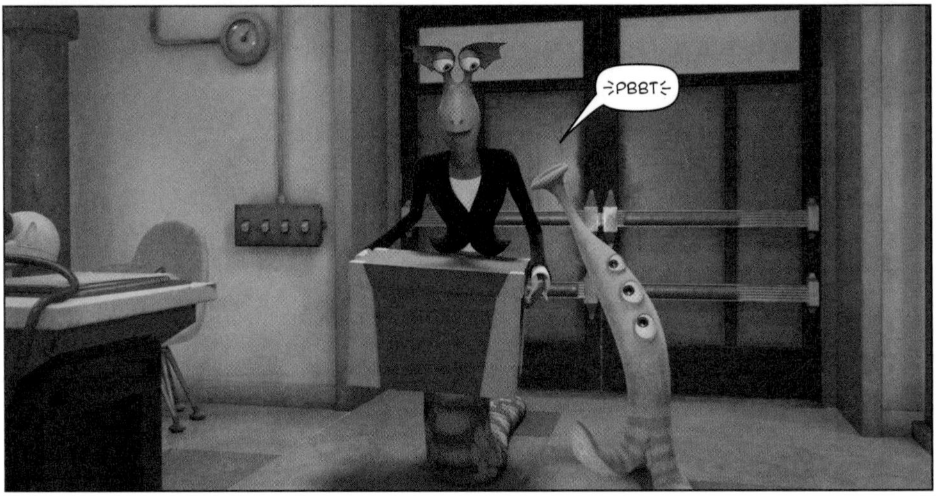
PBBT

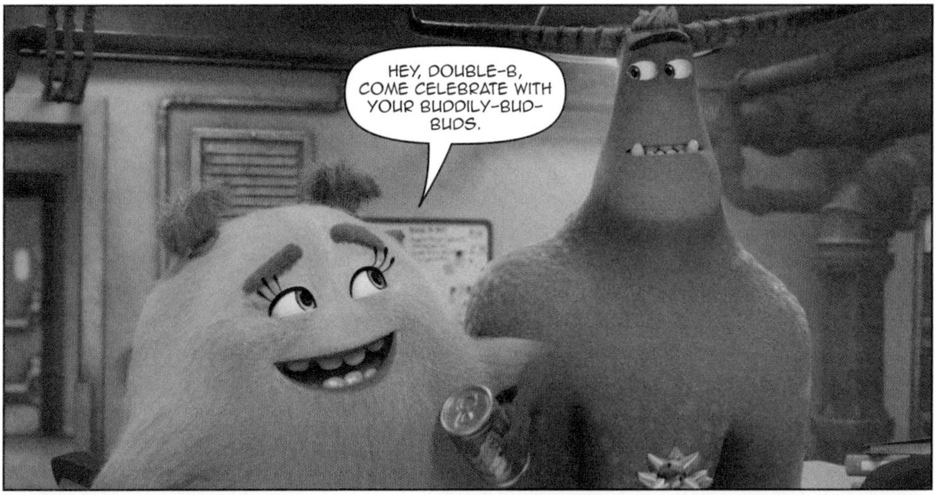
HEY, DOUBLE-B, COME CELEBRATE WITH YOUR BUDDILY-BUD-BUDS.

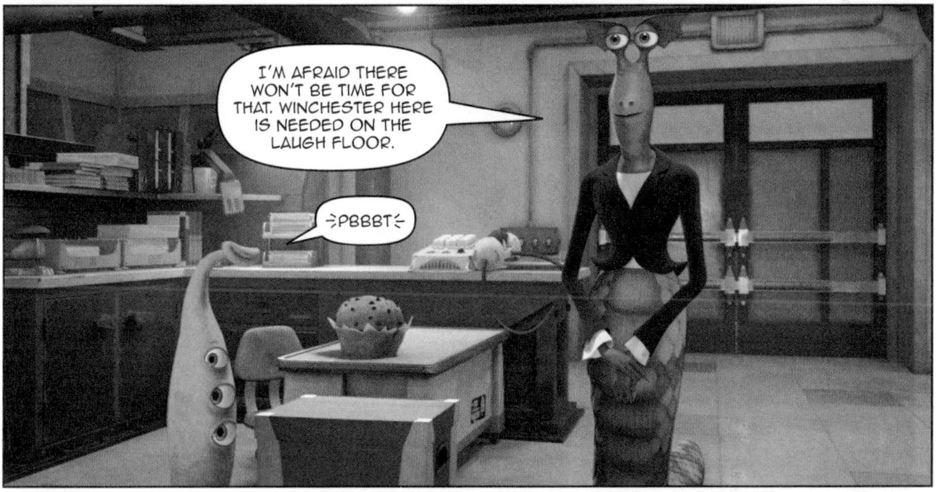
I'M AFRAID THERE WON'T BE TIME FOR THAT. WINCHESTER HERE IS NEEDED ON THE LAUGH FLOOR.
PBBBT

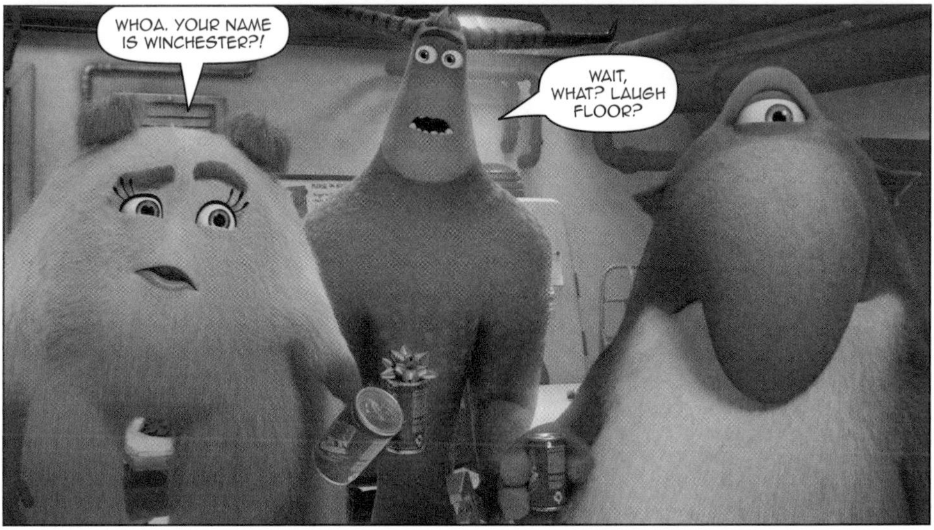
WHOA. YOUR NAME IS WINCHESTER?!
WAIT, WHAT? LAUGH FLOOR?

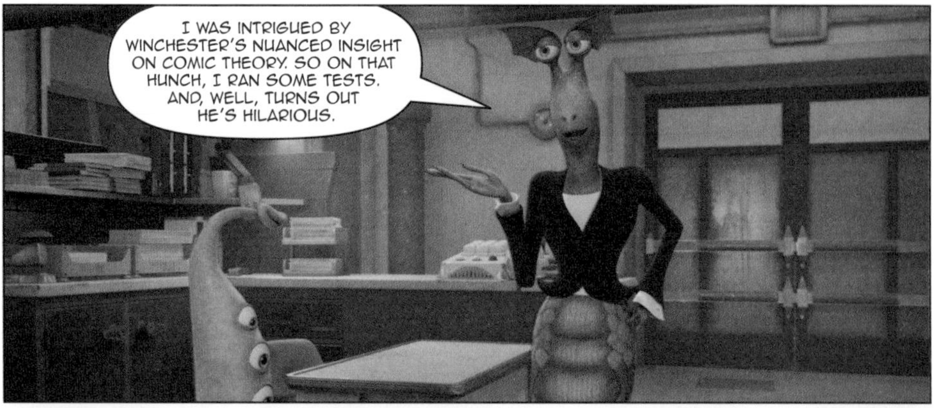
I WAS INTRIGUED BY WINCHESTER'S NUANCED INSIGHT ON COMIC THEORY. SO ON THAT HUNCH, I RAN SOME TESTS. AND, WELL, TURNS OUT HE'S HILARIOUS.

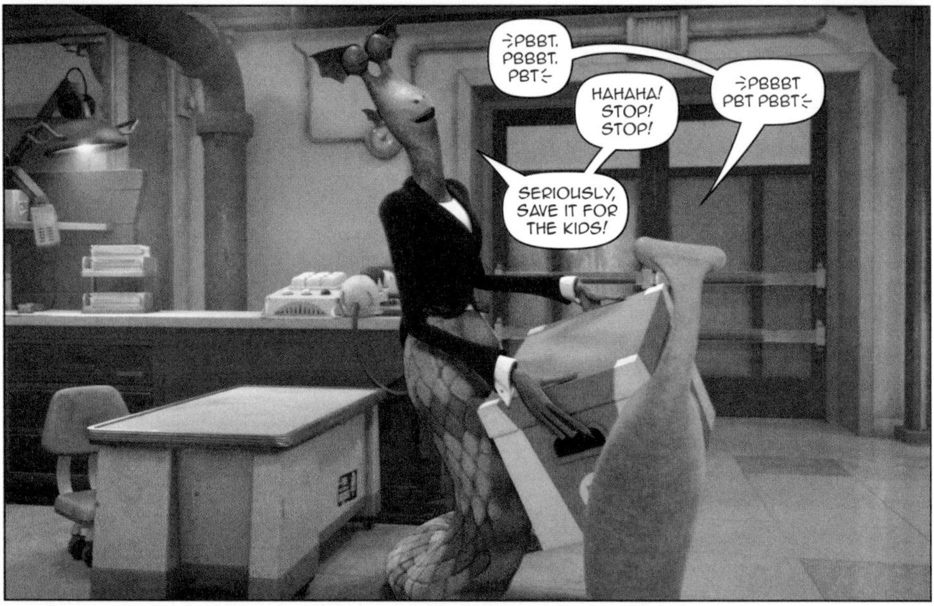
PBBT. PBBBT. PBT
HAHAHA! STOP! STOP!
PBBBT PBT PBBT
SERIOUSLY, SAVE IT FOR THE KIDS!

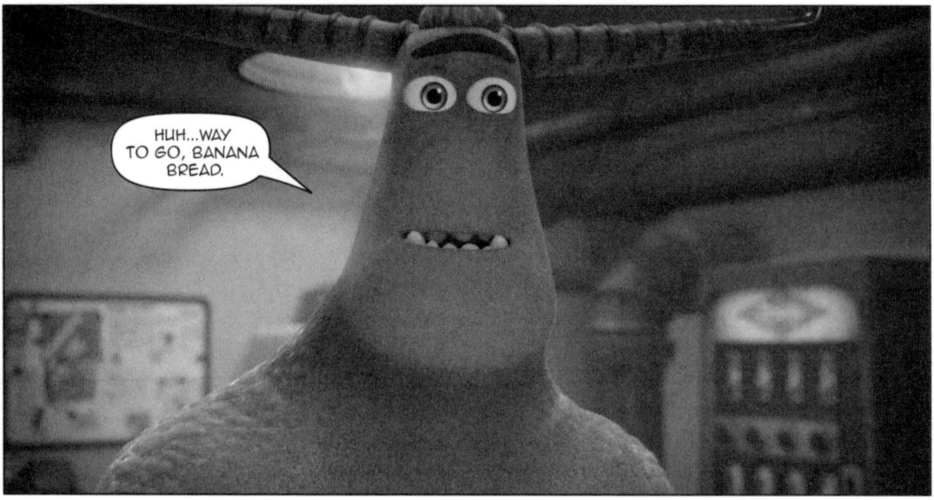
HUH...WAY TO GO, BANANA BREAD.

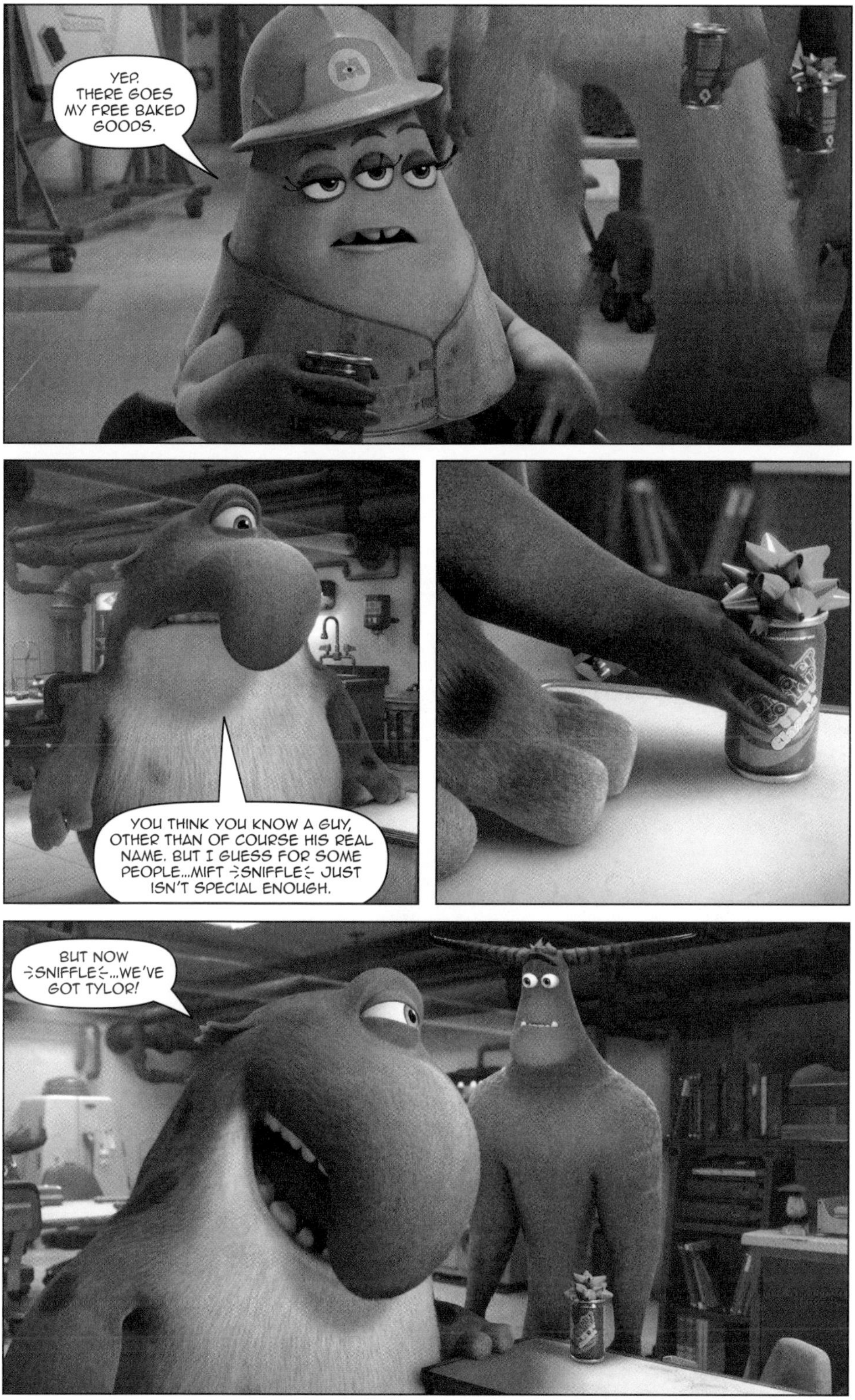
YEP. THERE GOES MY FREE BAKED GOODS.
YOU THINK YOU KNOW A GUY, OTHER THAN OF COURSE HIS REAL NAME. BUT I GUESS FOR SOME PEOPLE...MIFT →SNIFFLE← JUST ISN'T SPECIAL ENOUGH.
BUT NOW →SNIFFLE←...WE'VE GOT TYLOR!

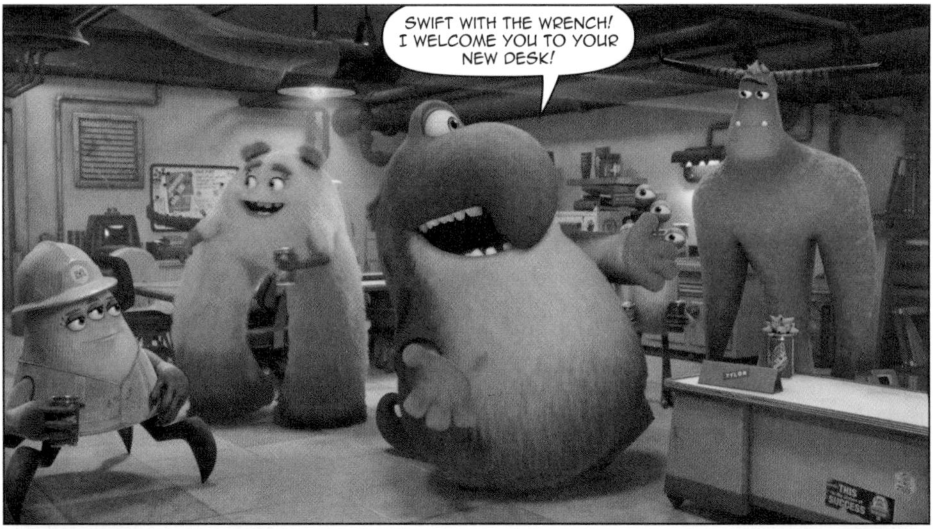
SWIFT WITH THE WRENCH! I WELCOME YOU TO YOUR NEW DESK!

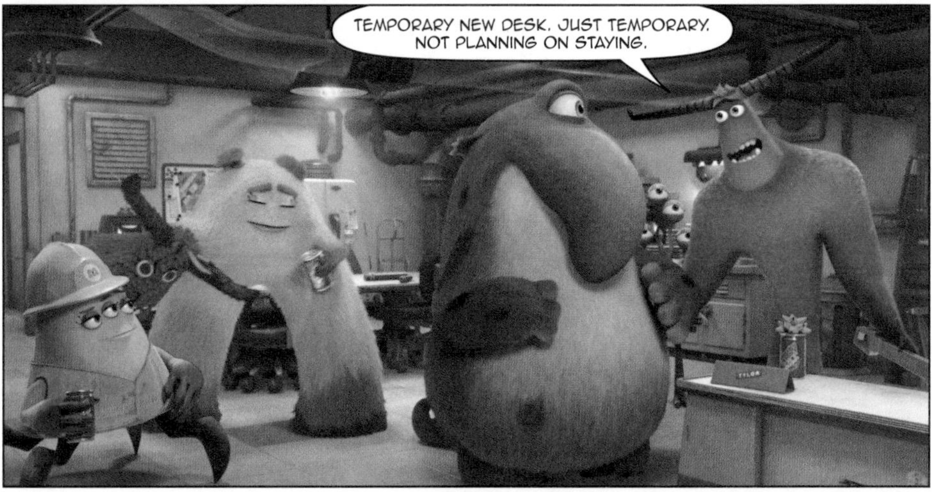
TEMPORARY NEW DESK. JUST TEMPORARY. NOT PLANNING ON STAYING.

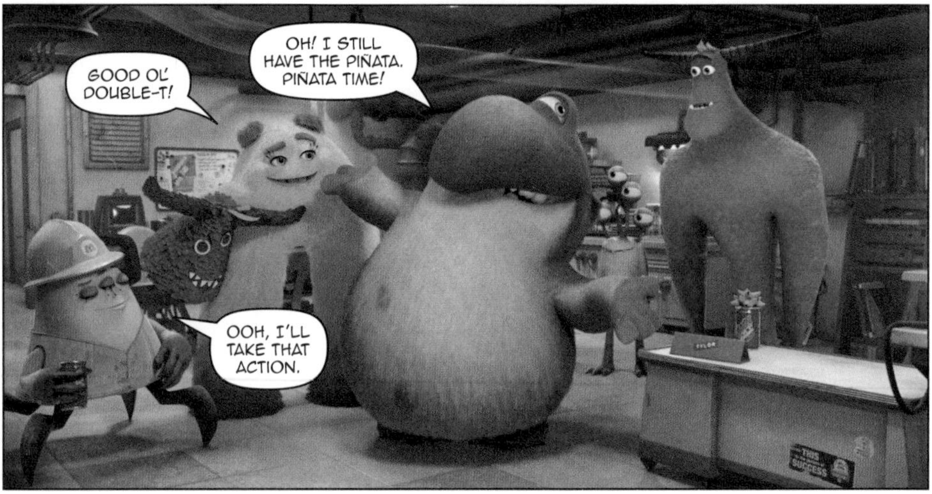
GOOD OL' DOUBLE-T!
OH! I STILL HAVE THE PIÑATA. PIÑATA TIME!
OOH, I'LL TAKE THAT ACTION.

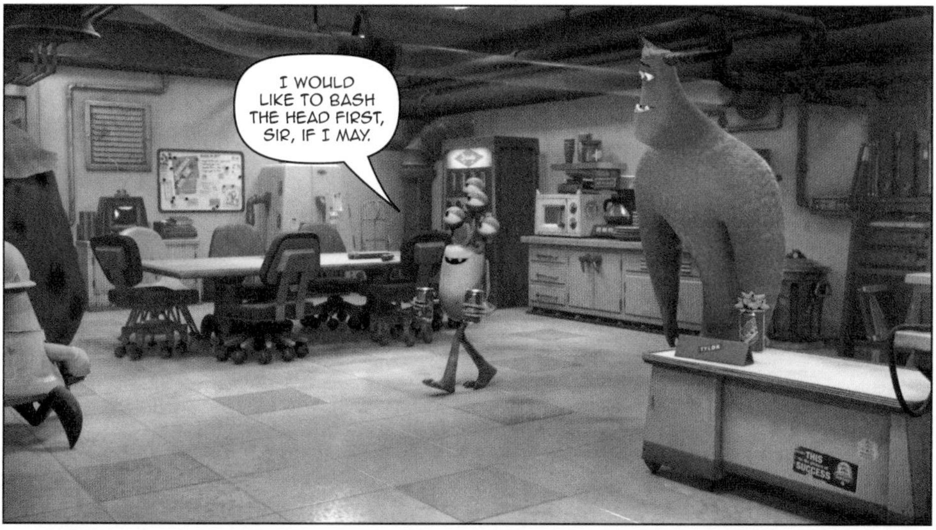
I WOULD LIKE TO BASH THE HEAD FIRST, SIR, IF I MAY.

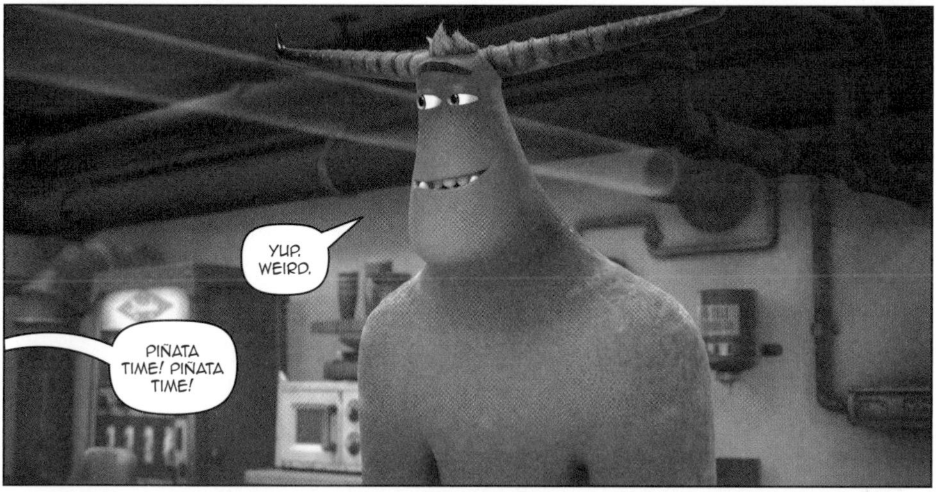
YUP. WEIRD.
PIÑATA TIME! PIÑATA TIME!

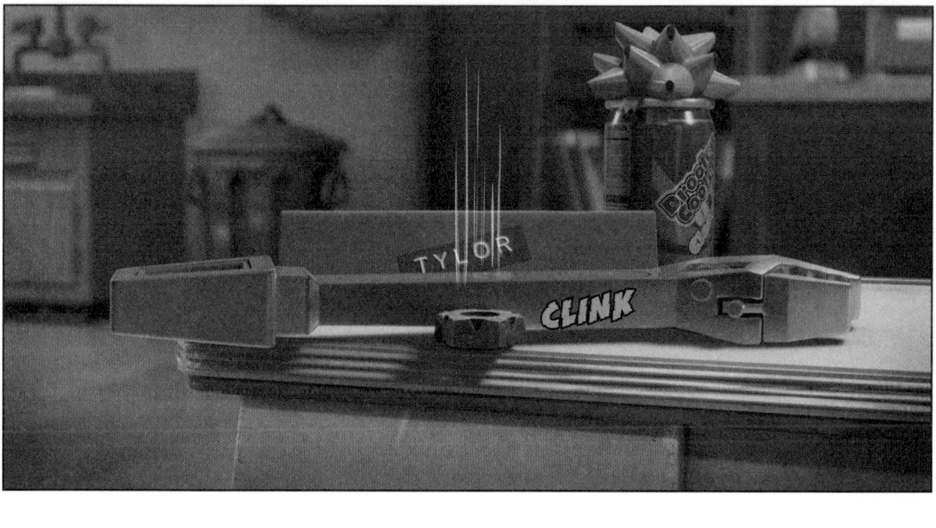
TYLOR
CLINK

DISNEY

MONSTERS AT WORK

Meet MIFT

Written by Bart Jennett
Directed by Shane Zalvin
Produced by Sean Lurie and Ferrell Barron
Executive Producer: Bobs Gannaway